Giselle
The Secret of the Locket

Meet the girls of Charlotte Bay

ESMERALDA LOPEZ 18
(EZI)

KATHERINE ANDERSON 17
(KIKI)

EMILY ANDERSON 17
(EM)

GISELLE HAYES-BRAY 16
(GI)

SOPHIE HAYES 16
(SOPH)

SILVER TAYLOR 15
(SILV)

Giselle
The Secret of the Locket

Maes E. and Stephanie G.

5 Sisters Ministry

Brisbane, Australia

"The name of the LORD is a strong tower;
the righteous run to it and are safe."

—PROVERBS 18:10

Prologue

The sound of shattering glass woke Giselle up. Terrified and disoriented, she sat up and looked around. She blinked hard to focus her sleepy eyes on her surroundings. Where was she?

She jumped as a crash of thunder echoed in the eeriness of the night. With a trembling hand she reached for her bedside lamp but grasped only air.

A flash of lightning lit the room, jolting her sleepy brain. Oh, it was Grandmama's house, but why was she wet?

A cool splatter of raindrops slapped Giselle's arms and legs. She remembered leaving the window wide open to drown the stifling heat. Now rain forced its way into the cosy room. Trembling a little, she scrambled out of bed and darted across the room to close the window.

She yelped as she stubbed her little toe on the corner of the bedside table. In the pitch black, she banged the window shut and limped across the room to turn the light on. As she reached for the light switch, a sudden explosion of thunder reverberated through the house. Terror-stricken, Giselle crouched down and covered her ears. She was unable to move or reach for the light switch.

Another outburst boomed through the house. With her heart pounding and tears threatening, she crawled to the door and fumbled with the doorknob until she managed to swing it open. The faint glow of the nightlight in the corridor greeted her thumping heart. Her quivering legs miraculously held her up as she ran to Sophie's room for safety.

"Soph, Soph!" Giselle cried as she burst into her cousin's room and turned on the light.

"What? What?" Sophie sat up and rubbed her eyes. Another clap of thunder resonated through the house. Once more, Giselle covered her ears and shut her eyes.

"The storm!" Giselle's voice squeaked.

Sophie jumped out of bed, her long blonde hair ridiculously tousled as she rushed to Giselle's side. "Gi, it's okay," she said. "You're safe with me and Grandmama. You'll be fine."

Still shaking, Giselle flopped onto her cousin's bed. "I'm such a baby! I mean, who is afraid of storms? I hate feeling like this. I hate it!" She covered her face with her hands and cried.

Giving her cousin a squeeze, Sophie whispered, "Really, Gi, everyone is scared of something."

"Yeah, maybe. But a storm? I'm not two, Soph!" Giselle burst out.

Lightning and thunder rumbled as if it were in the room with them. Giselle buried her head on her cousin's shoulder. Sophie hugged her, but she didn't say anything until the sounds started to roll away.

"Hey, that one wasn't that loud." Sophie smiled. Giselle could tell she was trying to ease her fears.

Giselle looked up, cocked her head, and listened intently as the roll of thunder and the brightness of lightning became more distant and softer yet still heavy rain pelted the roof and windowpanes. Rain was okay, though. Giselle loved rain.

Giselle slowly exhaled. She had not even realised she'd been holding her breath. Thank goodness Sophie had been around. She would probably have passed out if she had been on her own!

Chapter 1

Dear Diary,

I'm sooo tired but happy. We've been super busy the last few days hanging out with Grandmama. She took us to church and afterwards to have high tea at Valentina's Tearoom. The delicacies were mouthwatering, but they're so posh there. I wasn't allowed to wear my boho sandals, and Silver wasn't allowed to wear her cute cowgirl boots. Even Em wasn't allowed to wear the new Nike sneakers she had bought. It was torture wearing heels. Plus, my feet are long, and the pair I was wearing from my cousins were too tight. Squishing my feet into Sophie's little heels, I felt like one of Cinderella's ugly stepsisters. LOL. Sophie promises we are the same shoe size, but I don't think so. Hmm. Oh, and Grandmama took us to Crest Pointe Markets. That was dreamy! The things I found were awesome—some real cheapo stuff too.

Anyways, today's the big day when the family arrives for the end-of-January celebration. Everyone's going to be here—even Aunty Jackeline and Uncle Logan are here all the way from the USA. Silver is over the moon that her whole family made it. I feel like I have tons of family. So, let me break it down for you.

Nonno and Grandmama had five children: Miriam, Yasmin, Jackeline, Lousiana (my mum!), and Michael.

Then they had my cousins:

Miriam & Alex Lopez had Esmeralda.

Yasmin & Cameron Anderson had Nicholas, and then Katherine, Josh, and Emily (the last three are triplets!).

Jackeline & Logan Taylor had Ruby, Silver & Jade.

Lousiana & Warren Bray had me, Giselle, of course!

Michael & Celeste Hayes had Sophie.

There's sooo many of us. But as awesome as it is having all my aunts, uncles, and cousins, I wish my Nonno was here. My heart hurts so much when I think about him. He was the world's most amazing grandpa. I love that he left us this end-of-January tradition. I can still hear him saying, "We are family and no matter where we come from, we will always be one. We celebrate love, life, and bond." Then we would all click our glasses filled with grape juice and cheer. He's forever in my ♥! Today is the first time we celebrate since he passed away.

The next few hours will be nuts as we run around setting up the outdoor area with lights, music, flowers, and Nonno's favourite Mediterranean dishes he brought back from Italy. Anyways, I already hear the craziness of everyone running around outside, and I hear Soph calling my name. Oops, I better get moving. I can't wait for tonight to start!!

—G

Giselle drew a simple sketch of the heirloom dishes at the bottom of the page and smiled, satisfied with her drawings. Yep, they looked super cute. She shut the pages of her handmade floral-design journal with a thud. A diary entry was never complete without one of her drawings to beautify the page. She hid the eco-friendly book under the pillow and walked out of her room to meet the chaos.

"Giselle, I was going nuts looking for you!" Sophie grabbed Giselle by the arm and pulled her towards the back door and down the path towards Nonno's man cave. "Where were you?" she demanded, her usual perfect complexion flushed and drenched in sweat. "Never mind! Come help me find the fairy lights to decorate outside. I need to find those lights, or everything will be ruined! I've looked everywhere. Grr."

Giselle suppressed a smile at seeing her cousin in such a frenzy. Where had the impeccable, put-together Sophie gone?

"Soph, hold on." Giselle pulled her cousin towards her. "You need to chill, or you'll pass out. Breathe in, breathe out, and relax." Giselle closed her eyes and demonstrated how to breathe in and out slowly. "Like this," she said.

Sophie twisted her lip to one side and shook her head, "I don't have time . . ."

"Just do it. You'll feel tons better." Giselle didn't let go of her hand until Sophie started to breathe in and out at a slow pace.

A few seconds later, Sophie's blue eyes popped opened. "Ah," she said. "Thanks, Gi. I do feel tons better."

"Seeee!" Giselle squeezed her cousin's hand. "Okay, so exactly what are we looking for?"

"I need to put up the fairy lights, and Grandmama thinks they're in Nonno's shed . . . well, his man cave."

Giselle's stomach twisted when she saw Nonno's little green shed at the back of the garden. Outside of the shed was a garden chair and table. A few potted plants filled with Aloe Vera were on the other side.

Her heart beating a little faster, Giselle paused and took a deep breath. She remained quiet as Sophie talked on and on about how she was going to hang the lights.

The leafy trees above them moved gently with the breeze, and Giselle shivered involuntarily.

When they stopped at the little green-and-white wooden door, Sophie paused and turned to look at Giselle. Slowly, she turned the handle.

"Oh, Nonno, I miss you!" Sophie said out loud.

Giselle touched the door pane and smiled. She had helped him paint the door one hot summer's day. He had brought home a bunch of green paint palettes, and together they had chosen Hunter Green.

She laughed when she saw the crooked green streaks near the white paint. She had told Nonno to paint over her work, but he refused. He said he loved her artistic lines. Giselle shook her head. Only Nonno would say something like that.

"I haven't been in here for so long." Sophie's voice interrupted Giselle's thoughts as they walked through the door and into the dark stuffy room.

"Me either," Giselle whispered as she fumbled with the light switch and brought life into the room.

"Okay, you tackle that side of the room, and I'll look on this side. Hopefully he left those lights in here somewhere." Sophie wiped her hands on her white shorts, removed her sandals, and got down on her hands and knees to look inside boxes.

Giselle stared around the room and felt tears coming. In one corner was his striped sofa, his TV that looked like it belonged in the '60s, and an old record player that he loved. Giselle could almost hear his Italian folk music blaring throughout the shed. Beside a sink was a long bench where he kept some of Giselle's paints and a bookshelf. Giselle gasped when she spotted something on the bookshelf. She walked towards it and grabbed the tiny easel that sat gathering dust.

"Oh, wow, Soph, check this out." Giselle walked over to Sophie and showed her the tiny easel. "I painted this for Nonno ages ago. I can't believe he kept it."

Sophie grabbed the little easel and said, "Aw, how adorable. It's you and Nonno. Gi, you were an awesome artist even then. This is cool!"

Giselle giggled. "Thanks." She touched the painting with her index finger and sighed.

"This place is too dark. I'm going to go and get a torch to see better," Sophie said as she headed out the door. "I'll be right back." With those words she disappeared.

Giselle looked at the painting one more time and shook her head. Such good memories. She went to the bookshelf to put the little painting back in its place. Just as she set it down, her eye caught the title of a book. Giselle gasped as she read *The Count of Chateau Laurent.*

Suddenly her heart thundered in her chest, her throat tightened, and her breathing accelerated as she remembered that awful day three years ago.

Chapter 2

Three years earlier, a few days before Nonno passed away.

Giselle locked her mint-and-white retro bike with the chain, gave it a tug, and hurried up the steps of Crest Pointe Rest Home where Nonno lived. She patted her boho satchel that hung on her shoulder to make sure she could still feel her art journal and chocolate-filled croissants she was about to sneak to Nonno. She giggled. He always expected a treat when she came to visit.

She opened the door to the reception area and said, "Hi," to Jessica, the receptionist. Jessica's dark hair hung wavy and long across her shoulders. She was always glad to see Giselle.

"Welcome back, dear," Jessica replied.

Giselle smiled. "I came to show Nonno my latest art journal. He loves looking at it." She shifted her heavy bag to the other shoulder. "How is he today?"

Jessica looked around and lowered her voice. "He has had an off day." She pursed her lips. "Are you sure you want to see him like that?"

Giselle nodded. "Yes, please. I really want to see him."

"I tell you what," Jessica said, her smile warm and comforting. "I'll get you to sign in, and then if he's not himself, you can ring the bell, and the nurses can look after him. Sound like a plan?"

Giselle swallowed, her voice barely a whisper. "Okay."

After signing in, Giselle followed the blue tartan carpet all the way to room 203. She knocked softly on the door and turned the handle. Nonno's face was turned towards the window. She wasn't sure if he'd heard the door because he didn't turn around.

She took a deep breath. "Ciao, Nonno," she called out, loud enough to snap him from wherever his brain was.

Nonno's head swirled around, and a huge grin danced on his face. "If it isn't my little da Vinci!" He held out his arms.

Giselle almost cried with relief; he remembered her today. She rushed into his arms and held him tightly, taking in the familiar sandalwood smell of his soap. She inhaled—*mmm*—woody, earthy, creamy.

Nonno eyed her satchel. "My little Giselle, what have you painted for me?" he asked, scooting over on his bed to make room for her.

"Well," she began as she opened her satchel and took out her heavy, A4-sized art journal, "I have been painting something awesome." She pulled the book out and opened to her latest creation. "Ta-da!"

Nonno's mouth formed an *O*. "That's a remarkable painting, my little da Vinci. You have captured the essence of it impeccably. You are truly an impressive young artist. I salute you!" He bowed his head.

Giselle dissolved into laughter. He always critiqued her art with his best art critic voice and fancy big words.

His light brown eyes shone. "So, do I get a treat?"

She nodded and covered her lips with her index finger. "Shh, Nonno. I don't want the nurses to tell Grandmama." She took out the brown baker's bag and showed him the sweet goodness.

He opened the bag and giggled like a child. "I will have this with my coffee tonight," he promised.

For the next hour, Giselle filled Nonno in on the latest at school and on Mum, Grandmama, and the cousins. She noticed he was quiet. At times, he nodded, but other times, his eyes shifted from side to side, and occasionally, he wringed his hands. Giselle frowned, then shook it off. Maybe she had imagined his unease.

"Oh, and the twins told me to say hi," Giselle said as she placed her art journal back in her satchel.

Nonno's wrinkled brow deepened. "Who?"

Giselle's head snapped up. "You know, Emily and Katherine, the twins? I mean the triplets with Josh."

Nonno shook his head. "I don't know them. Do I?"

Giselle paused, took a deep breath. "Nonno, it's getting late, I have to get going." She touched his arm and tried to smile. She felt the light mood had shifted to a heavy one in seconds.

Nonno tapped a finger on his hand. "I don't remember who they are. Do I know them? Did I tell them a lie too?" He repeated the sentence a few times, the tap of his finger on his hand growing faster each time.

Giselle frowned. *Lie? What lie?*

She leaned over and gave him a quick kiss on the cheek. "Bye, Nonno. I love you." Her voice shook a little as she bolted from the scene.

"Rosie. Rosie, wait!" he shouted to her.

Giselle bolted back inside. "It's me, Nonno, Giselle, remember?"

His eyes were now glazed over. "Rosie, forgive me. Please forgive me."

Giselle frowned. Why did he call her by Grandma's nickname? She dumped her bag onto the ground and ran to his side, covering his hand with hers. "It's okay, Nonno. It's okay."

He was agitated, and tears streamed down his wrinkled face, a face she adored.

"I kept the locket, Rosie. I kept it. I couldn't get rid of it. I kept it for her. I kept it for her."

Giselle stared at her Nonno in utter confusion. *What locket?*

"I lied to you. Forgive me, Rosie." He babbled on and on, and then he said, "Darling, read my book, read my book."

Giselle leaned over and whispered, "What book, Nonno?" Her voice barely audible.

"Read my book, my book. Read *The Count of Chateau Laurent*." He grabbed her arm and pressed his fingers into her soft skin. "Promise me, Rosie. Promise me!" He was hysterical by now.

Frantic, Giselle pressed the emergency bell, and in an instant doctors and nurses rushed in, ready to calm him with medication.

"Honey, it's better if you leave." A nurse touched her arm sympathetically.

Giselle cleaned her tear-streaked face and nodded. She picked up her satchel and headed to the door.

"Read my book!" he screamed.

Just as the nurse pushed her out the door, Giselle made a mad dash to his side and cried, "I forgive you, and I will read the book."

He exhaled, and his eyes began to flutter as the sedative took effect. "Thank you," he managed to mutter, "Thank you . . . Giselle." Her name only a breath as he closed his eyes.

Giselle gasped at the sound of her name, and fresh tears streamed down her cheeks. By the time she reached her bike, she was sobbing uncontrollably. She sat on the concrete and cried until no tears came out. Her ribs and her throat ached.

As the last ray of sunlight started to disappear behind the mountains, she watched the sun sink and give its last rays for the day. Deep down she knew she had seen her Nonno alive for the last time.

Giselle shook her head as the horrible memories invaded her thoughts. She wiped her eyes and turned her back so Sophie wouldn't see her when she returned. Giselle had buried that traumatic day and hadn't remembered the book until now. Her hands shook as she reached for the book and picked it up. Little flakes of dust floated through the air and made her cough. Something felt off with the book; it was light. She turned it over and gasped. It wasn't a real book after all—it was hollow.

"It's a box!" she exclaimed. She opened the lid and saw a velvet pouch. Her fingers trembled as she picked it up and was about to open it when Sophie popped back in.

"Guess what?" Sophie said. "Kiki found the lights in the garage."

Giselle shut the lid in a hurry. "No way! Let's go set them up." She wiped her cheeks one more time and pretended to laugh.

"Uh, did you find a book?" Sophie said, pointing to the book under Giselle's arm.

Giselle nodded. "Yeah, to read at night," she lied.

The girls headed out, and Giselle bolted the door. She ran her hand down the front of the door and sighed.

Sophie, oblivious to Giselle's state of mind, babbled about going back to school, her new uniform, and her dad's business trip to England.

Giselle remained silent, lost in tangled thoughts.

As soon as she got in the house, she bolted to her room and hid the hollow book in her satchel. She would have to wait until she was home on Monday night to see what was inside Nonno's mysterious box.

Chapter 3

Dear Diary,

We had a blast this weekend. It was one of the best weekends we've had in a long time. We had so much food I could not move for hours. LOL. Except Emily, who ate enough to feed a zillion people, but she was like a bottomless pit, completely fine, and kept eating for us all.

Grandmama is an amazing cook, and she makes the yummiest vegetarian mock lamb. It was pretty much just for me 'cause I'm vegetarian, but everyone ended having some to "see what it tastes like"—they were jealous my 'lamb' looked divine.

I have to admit, there were times during the party I wanted to sneak away and open the hollow book. I have been dying to see what's in that pouch. It's been torture waiting, I couldn't even open it when I got home 'cause Uncle Mick and Sophie are home (well, it's a mansion not a home), and we ended up staying up with them. We sat outside on the veranda and watched the luxury yachts come in for the night. Uncle Mick has a beautiful yacht and sometimes takes Soph and me for a ride. Sometimes he goes on his own and spends a few days alone. He misses Aunt Celeste who died when Soph was little. You know, I'm always creeped out that Mum and Uncle Mick lost their spouses. I mean, Uncle Mick lost his wife, and Mum lost Dad, and to make it weirder still, Mum and Uncle Mick are twins! I know, super creepy. My biggest fear is to lose my mum. Gives me chills. Anyways, I'm going to bed soon—am so exhausted, but I need to open that pouch now! Otherwise, I'm going to go nuts.

—G

Giselle sketched a little pouch on the bottom of the page, shut her book, and reached for *The Count of Chateau Laurent*. Her hands trembled as she grabbed the pouch, drew the strings, and opened it.

Nestled safely inside was a locket. Giselle gently removed the locket and sucked in her breath. It was beautiful. The locket and chain were gold. A verdigris leaf was on one side with a delicate pink rose sitting on top, and the front of the locket was decorated with two beautiful green dragonflies. Engraved on one side were the initials O. A. B.

Slowly she opened the locket. Inside were two different black-and-white photos. The one on the left was a lovely blonde woman smiling, and on the right was a photo of a chubby baby laughing.

Giselle touched each photo carefully and wondered how Nonno knew this woman and baby.

She wondered who it belonged to and why Nonno had it. His words came floating back to her. *I kept the locket, Rosie. I kept it. I couldn't get rid of it. I kept it for her. I kept it for her.*

Had Nonno had an affair? Giselle's hand flew to her throat. Oh, Nonno.

She studied the photo a little longer and then closed the locket with a loud click. *Hold on, had she seen that woman before?* Giselle opened the locket again and studied the woman's face. The blonde hair and smile felt so familiar—had she visited Nonno at the house once? Or had she seen her at a park? Yes, that was it. The woman's face was hazy, but in her mind's eye she saw a beautiful woman with blonde hair at the park's playground. She had been swinging back and forth on the swings, and the woman had smiled at her.

Giselle closed the locket with a thud and tossed it back into its pouch. She couldn't handle the thought of Nonno having a love affair apart from Grandmama.

She bit her bottom lip and decided she needed to find out who this woman was. Giselle hoped his love affair had been before Grandmama.

But deep down she knew, it didn't sound right. She remembered seeing that woman before. There was no way she could tell her cousins or any of her family, especially not Grandmama.

The day was a little overcast, but Giselle could still see the ocean and the birds soaring above. They looked like they were migrating; the cooler days were approaching, after all. The air smelled like salt and fish mingled into one. She heard laughter all around her. Giselle paused and realised she was one of those chuckling. As she flew high on the swing, butterflies of delight danced in the pit of her stomach.

"Higher, Daddy! Higher, Daddy!" she squealed. Her father grinned.

He pushed her with one hand and fixed his glasses with the other. Suddenly, Giselle shrank back as female hands reached out to grab her. She gasped and tried to jump off the swing. She didn't recognise those hands. Fear gripped her heart as she wriggled desperately to get away from them.

"Don't touch me!" she screamed. "Don't touch me!"

Tears streamed down her face, and in her desperation, she looked for her father. Where was he? Hold on, was that Nonno? Giselle frowned. Then, suddenly, Nonno disappeared into thin air.

Again, the strange hands reached out and this time took hold of her waist and pulled her back.

Giselle screamed and woke up.

The dark, still night and the rapid beat of her heart stifled her. The chirp of a cricket under her window made her jump, and little goosebumps prickled her arms with the eeriness of the nightmare. She reached over and turned on her lamp. She said a little prayer and asked God to calm her heart.

Her legs wobbled as she hopped out of bed, opened her drawer, took out her headphones, and plugged them into her timeworn phone. She scrolled through her music playlist and soothed her anxiety with some peaceful worship music. The calm sound eased her soul, and soon she fell into a welcome yet restless sleep.

Chapter 4

Dear Diary,

I barely slept last night. That creepy dream made me jump each time I thought of that woman's hands. I don't know why her hands and her presence make me shiver. And why were my dad and Nonno in my dream. Super weird. I'm also completely intrigued by that locket I found. My heart hurts each time I think about Nonno having an affair. I have tried to think of other reasons, but nothing feels right. The affair seems to be the only explanation. I've hidden the pouch under my bed—there's a little ledge where it sits perfectly. I don't want Rosa, Uncle Mick's housekeeper who comes once a week, to find it. It needs to remain my secret … and Nonno's.

Anyways, at least I'm feeling better now. Having Sophie here has been sooo good. She goes back to school Thursday, which means I get her for another few days. I miss her so much when she's away. I wish she didn't have to go back to boarding school. I mean, I get the whole thing of Uncle Mick wanting to forget Aunty Celeste, but to send Sophie away so young seems cruel. He denies it, though, and says it's because he isn't home and can't look after her. But I know the truth.

I've seen photos of Aunt Celeste, and as Sophie gets older, she looks more and more like her. Seriously, they look like movie stars: blonde, blue eyes, tall, and just drop-dead gorgeous. Sometimes I look at my body and wish I had more curves. I'm tall and thin as a stick. Mum says I look so much like my dad. Even my dark hair and hazel eyes are like his. Anyways, I don't know why I'm even writing about my looks—maybe I'm nervous 'cause I'm starting senior year this year. So much pressure. I need to do well. I want to study art, have a studio, teach painting and drawing, and travel the world. How cool would that be? My dream is to go to Europe when I finish school. I think Europe would have the most amazing art culture in the world. Ah, just the thought paralyses me with joy. I need to save a ton of money to travel. Sophie wants to come with me—even Kiki and Emily. So, even though Europe has the best art, the real reason I want to go is because I need to visit my dad's grave in England. He was an English man. He's buried in Bristol, where I was born. Mum says that since Dad was very artsy, he loved Bristol because it's filled with music and history and culture. Dad was mostly inspired when he was in Bristol. He was an awesome painter. I've seen his work, but Mum keeps some in the garage safely covered.

Anyways, I better get ready for dinner. Uncle Mick is home, so the four of us are having dinner together. That barely happens, I can't wait!

I've been cooking up a storm with Sophie today. We love to cook but barely get time to do it. We've had a blast! Hope they like the food.

—G

Giselle sketched two chefs hats in the corner, closed her journal, and headed out the door. The delicious smell of roasted potatoes wafted to her room. Her stomach grumbled.

Downstairs, her mum was setting the table with Sophie, and soft music played in the background. Giselle paused at the bottom of the spiral staircase and watched them for a few seconds. They laughed about something one of them said, and Sophie eyes sparkled. Giselle wondered if Sophie was thinking about her mum.

Sophie lifted her blonde head and said, "Finally, the chef graces us with her presence." She laughed.

Giselle snickered and walked towards them. "Well, I had to change. I couldn't wear my clothes smelling like food. Besides, Emily and Kiki gave me this cute dress, and I had to wear it."

Mum looked her daughter up and down and wolf whistled. "Oh, honey, you look gorgeous. That's a beautiful dress. I love the one-of-a- kind embroidery."

Giselle twirled slowly. "It's the perfect summer dress, isn't it?"

Sophie nodded and said, "Plus, it shows off your figure." She winked.

Giselle let out a big loud cackle.

"I'm starved," Uncle Mick said, interrupting her laughter.

Giselle turned around and smiled. He was out of his business clothes and dressed in jeans and a T-shirt, still as handsome as ever. No one would know he was a millionaire dressed like that.

"Food is ready, Daddy," Sophie said.

"Yeah, we'll go serve." Giselle hurried to the kitchen as her mum followed close behind. "Hmm, Ma, please go sit down. I want to serve with Soph and spoil you and Uncle Mick."

Her mother tucked her short blonde hair behind her ear and grinned. "Sounds perfect to me." She winked and headed to sit with her twin at the dining table.

"Aunty Lusi is just the coolest," Sophie gushed as she took out the kebabs from the oven. "When I'm thirty-eight, like she is now, I want to look as good and go with the flow like she does."

"Yeah, I love her carefree spirit, Soph, but I wish she would settle down and find a great job." Giselle tucked an escaped strand of her hair into her side braid.

"She does have a job," Sophie said, then paused.

"Not anymore. She dumped it." Giselle pressed her lips together as she tossed the salad. "She lasts only about three weeks in each place. She doesn't really like anything."

Sophie chuckled softly. "That is totally true. I guess she hasn't found her thing."

Giselle placed the salad to one side and drizzled pesto over her roasted potatoes. "Yeah, I guess you're right. But the awesome thing is that she has an interview coming up. I hope this job sticks." Giselle cocked her head. She opened her mouth to continue but was interrupted by Uncle Mick's voice.

"We're starved! Is the food ready yet? I think I'm going to collapse!" he hollered.

Sophie and Giselle rolled their eyes and laughed.

"Daddy! You're such a baby," Sophie called back. She picked up the kebab tray and headed to the dining room. Giselle followed behind with the roasted potatoes in one hand and the salad bowl in the other.

"Giselle, you look like a pro waitress handling those dishes!" Sophie remarked as she set the kebabs down and took a seat.

Giselle winked and placed her dishes on the table. "I feel like one." She laughed.

Uncle Mick whistled and said, "This food looks delectable! Let's eat." He reached for a kebab.

Mum cleared her throat for attention "Not so fast, we're going to say grace first."

Everyone laughed.

Uncle Mick bowed his head and prayed the blessing.

"These kebabs are *delizioso*!" He took another bite, and the juice dripped down his chin.

Sophie giggled. "Daddy, you eat at the finest restaurants in the world. I'm sure you've eaten better kebabs in Istanbul or wherever."

"Soph does have a point," Mum added as she wiped her mouth.

"Yes, you're both right, but their food always lacks something." He paused.

Sophie and Giselle looked at each other and frowned. "What?" they asked in unison.

"Love." He smiled.

Giselle and Sophie burst out with laugher as Giselle's mum groaned.

"It's true!" Uncle Mick exclaimed. "It's like this." He moved his finger in a circle and pointed from Giselle all the way to his sister. "Us together. It's so good having home-cooked food and being with each other. Believe it or not, I miss it."

Giselle's heart ached for her uncle. Sophie reached out and grabbed his hand.

"When's your next trip, Mick?" Mum asked as she ate the last of her potatoes.

"I leave for England on Friday. I'll drop Soph at school on Thursday and then drive back and sleep at a hotel near the airport." He took a sip of his mineral water.

Giselle gasped, "Oh, Uncle Mick, I'm dying to go to England! I wish I could go with you."

"I would love for you to go along with me," he said.

Giselle shook her head. "Not now, though. I'm starting the eleventh grade in a few days and can't go anywhere."

Sophie pouted. "Gi, just wait till you finish the twelfth grade, and then we can go around Europe together."

Giselle squealed, and the girls grabbed each other's hands, "How cool will that be!"

"That's a wise plan," Uncle Mick began. "Start planning, and you can have the time of your lives. I might go with you girls to keep you safe." He laughed when Sophie's face paled.

"I actually have a plan," Giselle announced. She glanced at everyone around the table, taking special note of her mum's expressionless face and crossed arms.

22

Giselle frowned but continued. "I want to start working part-time so I can afford the trip by the end of my senior year. That'll give me two years to save."

"Europe is too expensive. You will need to save at least five years." Her mum's sharp tone burst her enthusiasm like little soap bubbles pricked by rough hands.

"Daddy could always pay," Sophie offered.

Giselle's mum lifted her hand when Uncle Mick opened his mouth. "No charity, Mick. I know you will offer to pay. If I send my daughter overseas, it'll be at my own expense."

"Mum, I don't expect you to pay," Giselle cried out. "I will save really hard, and I'll have plenty."

"I don't have a problem paying for Giselle," Uncle Mick stated.

Giselle's mum pointed her index finger at her brother and said, "Mick, you promised you wouldn't interfere with my decisions regarding Giselle. She isn't going and that's final!" She stood up abruptly, and the sound of a fork hitting the glossy marble titles rang out. She grabbed her plate and stormed towards the kitchen.

Giselle stared after her mum. She felt like the air had been sucked out of her soul.

Just as her mum was about to go through the door, she turned and stared straight at Giselle, her grey-green eyes narrowed, "I don't want you to work. Concentrate on your studies. Don't be a failure like me." With those words, she disappeared inside the kitchen.

Silence seemed to suffocate the room.

Her face burning, Giselle wrung her hands. She felt as if she'd been slapped across the face.

Chapter 5

Giselle felt tears gather in the corners of her eyes. She blinked rapidly and took a long, shaky breath.

Uncle Mick was the first one to speak. "Okay girls, I'm going to help Lusi clean the kitchen." He stood up and stretched. "I suggest you go for a long walk." He winked, grabbed a stack of plates, and headed to the kitchen.

Giselle turned to Sophie and whispered, "Let's go."

Sophie nodded and stood up abruptly.

Giselle tightened her arms across her chest and rubbed them briskly. The night air was a little crisp near the marina. Tiny lights reflected on the water and yachts, and somewhere in the distance, soft romantic music played.

"You okay, Gi?" Sophie's voice broke through her muddled brain.

Giselle nodded. "She was so mad, Soph. I have never seen her so angry." She shivered.

The girls continued their walk in silence. Finally, Giselle spoke again. "I mean, I get she doesn't have a steady income and can't send me. But I offered to work and pay for Europe. I have two whole years to save." Giselle exhaled, trying to let the wind take her frustrations away.

"It's not your fault, though," Sophie began. "She just doesn't want you to work and be—what did she say?—a failure or something."

Giselle shook her head. "But that's just it: she's not a failure, like she thinks. She got her Bachelor of Business degree at the university way before she met Dad."

"Did Grandmama force her to choose business? Was there some other subject she was interested in?" Sophie asked as they headed towards the town centre.

"No, she liked business, but she just couldn't figure out how to make a career of it." Giselle shrugged. "That's the story of her life." A wave of guilt washed over her. She didn't mean to talk harshly about her mum.

"Gi, I have a brilliant idea!" Sophie grabbed Giselle's arm and squeezed it. They stopped in the middle of the pathway.

The tingling of a bike bell sounded behind them, signalling for them to move.

"Sorry," Giselle called out and waved as a family rode past. She turned back to Sophie and asked, "What brilliant idea?"

"I can sell some of my jewellery and pay for your airfare! That way you don't have to work, and you'll keep the peace with your mum." Sophie let out a squeal. "Brilliant, right?"

"Soph, are you nuts? I mean, you're super sweet, but you can't get rid of them. They were your mum's!" Giselle watched as Sophie's eyes clouded over and her smile disappeared into the night.

"Oh, I forgot." She touched her delicate rose-gold necklace and turned to walk away.

Giselle groaned and ran to catch up with her. "Sorry, Soph, I didn't mean to upset you."

Sophie wiped her eyes and spun around. "Don't be silly, you didn't make me sad. It's just that sometimes I miss her so much that I can't breathe."

Giselle nodded, linked arms with Sophie, and said, "Let's go to Kim's Deli Café. I think a chocolate caramel bliss ball is in order!"

Sophie sniffled and gave a quick nod. "Sounds heavenly."

The girls walked towards their favourite café where the aromatic smell of wood-fired pizza, roasted nuts, fresh coffee, and light, happy music danced around them. It lifted their spirits, and soon the argument at the table and Aunt Celeste were forgotten, at least for the time being.

"Uh, I love the lights! They still haven't—" Giselle stopped to fix her Apache style sandal. "Ugh, these shoes are giving me blisters!"

"Where did you get them? They are pretty ugly." Sophie's mock-disgusted voice made Giselle groan.

"Gee, thanks, Soph." Giselle pretended to pout as she unclasped her shoes. "Actually, I found them at Crest Pointe Markets." She took her long feet out of the shoes and wriggled her toes in relief. "They were only two dollars. How could I not buy them?"

"They are also too small." Sophie wrinkled her delicate upturned nose. "I have a pair of gold sandals to die for. You can have them if you want."

"Soph, I don't need new shoes!" Giselle protested.

Sophie's baby-blue eyes twinkled. "Oh, but you'll love these! They are Tory Logans. Daddy got them for me last Christmas, but they are too big. I think they'll fit you, though."

Giselle didn't have a clue who Tory whoever was. Maybe they were some of those $300 sandals that were expensive but boring. No style. No feathers, shells, or colour to them. Then again, her feet were killing her. Maybe it wouldn't hurt to try them.

"I can buy them off you." Giselle picked up her shoes and walked barefoot on the cool yet rough concrete walkway.

"Nah, they're my gift to you." Sophie flicked her blonde tresses. "Anyways, back to helping you make money."

"Well, I was freaking out when Mum had that outburst, but this walk has helped, and I am going to get a job." Giselle pointed to Kim's Café as it came into view. "I'm going to work *there*!"

Sophie gasped. "What? How'd you know they need help?

"Well, remember when Silver was looking for a necklace for her bell pendant?" Giselle stopped in front of the big display window adorned with currently empty food platters.

Sophie looked through the window too. "Yeah. What about it?"

"There it is!" Giselle practically shouted as she grabbed Sophie by the arm and pulled her towards the sign. "We saw this when we came with the cousins." Giselle touched the words behind the glass and read it to

Sophie. "Part-time waitress needed. Drop your resume. Start ASAP!"

"Oh yeah, now I remember!" Sophie exclaimed. "Sorry to burst your bubble, Gi, but there's one problem."

Giselle's brow wrinkled. "What?'

"Since you're only sixteen, you need your mum's permission." Sophie patted her arm. "It won't work."

Giselle bit her bottom lip. "Uh, I've got it. It doesn't have to be mum; it can be another adult."

"Which adult?" Sophie turned to look at her. "Every member of our family is out. They'd tell your mum."

"I'll ask Rachel Craig. She's awesome. She'll do it." Giselle did a little dance. Rachel was the pastor's wife and her Bible Study mentor. "Gee, I'm brilliant," she said, laughing.

Sophie clapped. "Okay, perfect. You can ask Rachel tomorrow. Now, go in and ask about the job."

"Wish me luck!" Giselle pushed the door open, and the little bell above the door jiggled to announce their visit. She put on her shoes and grimaced as they scraped her bubbling blisters.

The smell of salami and coffee wafted through the air, and Giselle wriggled her nose in distaste. She didn't hate the smell as such, but the smell of meat made her nose sensitive. She took a deep breath and headed to the counter to ask for Kim.

Sophie whispered to her something about finding a seat, but Giselle's heartbeat drowned out her words.

Giselle said a quick prayer for strength and instantly felt shame. She was about to lie and had asked for God to help her.

"Can I help you?" The male voice behind her made her jump, and she spun around to see who it belonged to.

A guy with shaggy, sandy blond hair, gorgeous green eyes, and a knee-weakening smile was standing right behind her.

Giselle opened her mouth to speak, but no sound came out.

The guy grinned. "Hey, it's you! I know you," he exclaimed as he shifted his tray to his left arm.

Giselle gaped. "You do?" She squinted; he did look familiar. Did he go to her school? Maybe a year ahead of her?

"Yeah, I've seen you hang out here with a bunch of girls." He pointed to a booth. "And you always sit in that booth."

Giselle gasped. Should she be creeped out? He continued, "I've noticed you for a while. I'm glad I finally get to meet you." His cheeks dimpled as his voice and eyes softened.

Giselle's knees turned to jelly, and suddenly she needed to sit down. She grabbed onto a nearby table.

Finally, she broke her silence. "Oh, wow, okay. Thanks." She felt her cheeks flush. She hoped she didn't sound completely inept at making conversation. "Um, I . . . I was looking for Kim."

"She's in the back. I'll get her." He grinned one more time and disappeared to the back.

Giselle turned to Sophie, who sat at their usual booth. Giselle mouthed, "He's gorgeous!"

Sophie mouthed back, "Who is he?"

Giselle shrugged. She wasn't sure, but she sure wanted to know.

"Hi, I'm Kim. Can I help you?" At the sound of the female voice, Giselle turned around and smiled.

"Hi," she managed to say as she glanced behind Kim's shoulder to see where the cute guy had gone. She saw him near the counter. He looked at her, and their eyes met. Giselle glanced away and looked back at the owner.

"Oh, Giselle, it's you. How can I help?" Kim tucked part of her ash blonde hair behind one ear and motioned for them to move to the back of the café.

Giselle cleared her throat. "I was wondering about the sign at the door, the one about a part-time waitress."

"Are you interested in applying?" Kim opened a book and wrote down Giselle's name.

Giselle nodded. "Yes, please. I don't have a resume yet, but I can have it to you this week."

Kim placed the pen down and smiled. "Come by this Thursday at four for an interview."

Giselle inhaled sharply. "Really?"

"Yes, I've known you and your whole family for years. I know you are a good kid. Bring your resume with you." Kim took out a form from a drawer and handed it over to her. "I need this paper signed with your mum's signature giving you permission to work."

Giselle nodded slowly. "About that." She paused before saying, "My mentor, Rachel, from church is going to sign it. She's the pastor's wife. My mum is working all the time, and I never have time to catch her." She shifted uncomfortably from one sore foot to the other.

"No problem. That should work nicely." Kim smiled. "See you Thursday."

"Thanks again. See you then." Giselle gave a little wave and headed to where Sophie sat.

She plunked down into the chair and exhaled. "I've got an interview this Thursday after school! Yikes."

"Yes!" Sophie squealed softly. "You'll definitely get it."

"Thanks for the vote of confidence." Giselle glanced back to find the cute guy, but he wasn't around. Maybe he was in the back.

"So, who was that guy?" Sophie leaned forward and raised her eyebrows up and down. "He's cute."

Giselle lifted her shoulders. "I don't know, but he said he's noticed me before when I come with you guys."

"What?! He said that?" Sophie covered her mouth. "Tell me everything."

Giselle giggled, leaned forward, and whispered, "He said he's noticed me for a while and was glad to finally meet me."

Sophie clutched her own face with both hands. "Oh, Gi, too romantic!" She gushed.

Giselle nodded. She had an admirer. She couldn't believe it.

Chapter 6

Dear Diary,

What a day it's been. First it was awesome, then weird with Mum losing her mind, and then awesome again with a guy who might be crushing on me! Yikes. How is that even possible? I mean, no guy has ever liked me. Well, none I've known about. I have no curves whatsoever. My legs are long and skinny, no hips or curves. Flat as a surfboard. It feels strange knowing a guy likes me. Guys usually like curvy, sexy girls like Ezi or beautiful blonde babes like Sophie or cutie pies like the twins. Even Silver is stunning with her massive red hair and big grey eyes; plus, she has a bonus of an American twang.

On the way home, I called Rachel and asked her if she could fill out the permission paper for the job that I needed an adult to sign. She asked if Mum knew about this new job, and I lied and said yes. I feel so guilty. She's a pastor's wife; do you think maybe she'll find out I lied to her? She might have a vision showing me lying. I hate to lie, and I have never done anything behind my mum's back. But I can't tell her anything these days. She's already going ballistic about my plans to go to Europe. Soph reckons it's not lying 'cause I'm not telling her anything at all. Hmm, I don't know. Rachel is going to meet me after school at the library. I really need that job!

Anyways, when Soph and I got back from the café, we walked down the long hallway and heard muffled voices coming from Uncle Mick's study. I signaled for Soph to keep quiet, and we leaned our heads against the door. Okay, before you judge me, we weren't eavesdropping. Not really. I just had to hear if my mum was still mad or not. Anyways, their conversation went like this.

Uncle Mick: "I think you're overreacting."

Mum: "Overreacting?" (She choked.) "You know very well why Giselle can't go overseas. She needs a passport."

When I heard that, I looked at Sophie and rolled my eyes. I mean, obviously I'd need a passport if I was going overseas.

Uncle Mick: "A passport can easily be—"

Mum, interrupting him: "Mick!" (She was practically yelling.) "You know that's not the issue. She needs the documents, and I can't give those to anyone, especially to Giselle."

Uncle Mick, sighing: "Yeah, I forgot that little detail. What will you do?"

Mum: "I don't know. I'm thinking."

I heard someone stand up and move towards the door. Sophie and I bolted upstairs.

I don't get it. What document is she talking about? And why can't I have it? My head hurts. The fight, the cute guy, and the documents are making me nuts. Too much drama in one day.

I don't know if Mum will talk to me, but I hate her being mad at me. Maybe I should go talk to her. Okay, maybe not tonight. Probably in the morning.

I don't think I can handle another fight. Ugh. I'm off to sleep.

—G

PS. I hope I don't have the nightmare again.

Giselle sketched a broken heart in the bottom corner of the page and closed her journal with a thud. She prayed, reached over and turned off her lamp, then went to sleep.

The soft light of the morning sun peered through Giselle's window. The warmth caressed her face. Giselle stretched and popped one eye open. She smiled—no nightmare. Her smile disappeared quickly when she thought about her mum's outburst the night before. She grabbed her bed sheet and covered her face. She did not feel like arguing today. She was going to start school the next day and arguing unnerved her. She needed to get out of bed and exercise—that always made her feel a thousand times better. Giselle looked at her clock; it read 5:45 a.m. She got out of bed, dressed in her exercise clothes, and grabbed her devotional—to "start the morning right," as Nonno used to say. She sat on the window seat and basked in the silence of the house. Giselle read each page of her book and highlighted Bible passages that stood out to her.

By 6:10 a.m., she tiptoed downstairs with her backpack and headed to the garage to grab her bike. A wave of intense heat slapped her face as she mounted her bike and began peddling towards the lighthouse. Honestly, there was nothing pretty about summer. Sweat. Heat. Smells. Sticky legs. And just . . . yuck. Give her spring anytime.

Despite the day being hot so early, Giselle enjoyed her bike ride. She arrived at the lighthouse, locked her bike, and headed to her favourite shady area behind the lighthouse. A few people were doing exercises in different areas. She didn't mind, though, as long as the only thing she could hear was the water smashing against the rocks below.

Giselle took a deep breath as she admired the view. *Could the sky get any bluer?* she wondered. The water below seemed to call her name. She wished she could go for a swim and cool off. The "No Swimming" sign brought her back to the reality that she wasn't allowed to. Giselle shrugged, sat down on the cool green grass, and began to sketch.

The ding on her phone startled her. It was Sophie.

WHERE ARE YOU? the text read.

When Giselle looked at the time—8:30—her eyes widened. She had been gone for over two hours. She texted quickly: WENT RIDING—GOING HOME NOW. SEE YOU SOON. X.

She shoved her things into her backpack and journeyed home.

By the time she arrived, Sophie was having a shower and Uncle Mick was on a business call.

Giselle ran up the marble staircase to take a shower but decided to stop by her mum's room first. She didn't want to start the day with the awkwardness from last night. She stood at the door for a few minutes and heard rustling inside. She inhaled and knocked softly. "Ma?"

"Come in." Her mother's voice sounded a bit muffled, like she was in her walk-in wardrobe.

Giselle opened the door tentatively and stuck her head in. "Are you decent?" she asked.

She didn't see anyone, but she heard her mother laugh. "Yes."

Giselle exhaled—Mum sounded in a better mood. She plopped down on the bed, cleared her throat, and began the speech she had practiced earlier. "Ma, I'm sorry I made you mad last night. I didn't mean—"

"Oh, honey." Her mum hobbled out of the walk-in wardrobe with one black high heel on and struggling to put the other one on. "It's my fault. You have done nothing wrong. I overreacted. Sorry, honey." Her mum stopped in front of her and gave her a kiss on the head.

Giselle smiled. "You're probably nervous about your interview," she said.

She nodded. "I woke up so nervous, I didn't even have breakfast. I'm truly over interviews, hon. I hope this job is the one."

Giselle hoped so too. Her mum had moved from job to job for years. She often said she hated everything she applied for. Hopefully, today was the day she would settle down. Giselle watched her mum put her shoe on, sit down at her vanity table with a mirror, and start to apply mascara.

"Your uncle Cameron was so amazing to recommend me to his boss. He is my angel." She ran the black goo over her lashes. Giselle cringed. If she had to wear makeup for some reason, she'd rather just wear some lipstick.

Giselle was thankful to Uncle Cameron for arranging this interview. She would have to tell Emily and Kiki how amazing their dad was. "So, what time is the interview?" Giselle looked at her phone.

"It's at 10:30. What's the time now?" Her mum closed her mouth as she applied a lovely shade of burgundy to her lips.

"You still have plenty of time. It's only 9:05." Giselle admired the colour and made a mental note to find something like that in a paint colour. She could see it on her artwork.

Her mum screwed the lipstick cap back in place, then took off her robe. She admired herself in the mirror one last time and stood up. "Well?" she said, twirling for her daughter.

Giselle gave a thumbs-up. "Love everything. Except . . ." She paused and tilted her head to one side. Her mum looked great, wearing formal black pants and a white silk blouse, her hair in a sophisticated bun. Giselle wondered how on earth she had been able to create a bun with her short bob.

"Except what?" her mother asked with a tinge of panic in her voice.

"Mum, chill." Giselle walked to her mum's dresser and opened the top drawer where she kept some beautiful brooches.

"You need colour, and I think this brooch that Dad gave you will look stunning." She reached over to pin it onto her mum's blouse.

"No!" her mum cried and moved back to avoid the pin.

Giselle frowned. "What's wrong?"

Her mum stared at her blankly for a few minutes before she blinked. "It could fall off, and then I'll lose it. I can't risk losing that brooch." She touched the top of her blouse. "Maybe I can wrap a scarf."

Giselle nodded and went back to put the cute, yellow daisy pin in the drawer. The daisy looked exactly like the ones her dad had painted years ago. That's how they had met. Her mum was at an art festival in Amsterdam with some friends. She went to her dad's little booth where he exhibited his work and ran some workshops. Her mum saw a gorgeous painting of a vase filled with daisies. She fell in love with the vase and soon with Giselle's dad. She said his English accent made her weak at the knees. Three months later they married. Grandmama was horrified. She had not gone to the wedding. She was opposed to her daughter marrying a man she barely knew. Nonno and Uncle Mick had gone to the wedding, and a year later Giselle was born.

"What do you think?" Her mum's voice interrupted her thoughts. Giselle shut the drawer and turned to look at her mum as she completed her outfit with a delicate wildflower scarf.

"You look gorgeous, Mum, and very much like a flight attendant." Giselle walked over to her and straightened one side of the scarf.

"Except I won't be a flight attendant," she said. "My interview is for booking flights and things like that. I'd be a receptionist for the airline Cameron works at." She grabbed her purse and took a deep breath. "I'm ready."

Giselle grinned. "When the interviewer person sees you, he will give you an air hostess job for sure."

Her mum laughed and walked out the door, and Giselle followed her down the hallway. A beep outside made them both jump. "Taxi!" Giselle and her mum exclaimed in unison.

They laughed and hurried downstairs. Uncle Mick was still on his phone call, but he covered the mouthpiece and whispered, "Good luck, Peter Pan."

Giselle always laughed when he called her mum by his nickname for her. Her mum rolled her eyes and stuck out her tongue at him. "I'm grown up now," she mumbled as she opened the door. Her mum paused, turned to Giselle, and said, "Please say a little prayer for me. I need it."

"I will, Ma. You'll be fine." Her mum reached to give her a hug and a kiss, but Giselle moved back. "I smell like sweat. I went riding."

"Oh, okay then." She blew her a kiss and disappeared into her taxi.

Giselle stood at the door and watched the car drive down the gravel road and out the gate. She sighed. "God help Mum do well, please," she said in a whisper, adding, "and please help her love this job so she will stay with it."

She also needed her mum to be busy at work so she could work at Kim's Deli Café—if she got the job.

Giselle went back inside the elegant house and went upstairs to get ready for the day.

Her stomach did a little somersault when she thought about going back to school the next day. She didn't feel ready.

Chapter 7

Dear Diary,

Today is the day. First day back to school and Year 11. I'm freaking out. I honestly feel sick, and I want to crawl into a hole and hide forever. My heart is beating like crazy.

I texted my best friends, Indigo and Quinn, last night, and they're as nervous as I am. Phew. Glad it's not just me. I just want the day to be over and done with.

Actually, I want the whole week to be over and done with. I have my job interview tomorrow after school, and I see Rachel today so she can sign the paper. I hate to lie. Maybe I should just tell my mum. Okay, I can't do that. Maybe I should just listen to her and forget all about this work business. In two years I can get a loan from Sophie and we can go together. That'll work. Won't it?

Ah, no, it will not! What am I thinking? I can't get Soph to pay for me. Okay, plan B. I start working part-time, and then I will tell mum after the first week. I won't lie to her about it. Yep, that's it. I'll tell her next week.

Phew, that feels much better! Okay, okay, maybe I'm a wimp, but I'm happy I won't continue lying to her.

All right, enough about that. I'm going to get ready for school and head to Kim's Café. All the cousins will be there. I can't wait to see them.

It's tradition that we meet at the beginning of each school term—we have breakfast together and then we all go our own way.

It's already 7:00 a.m., so I'd better scurry and head off with Soph.

By the way, Mum's interview went well. She said she was interviewed by a man and a woman, and they were really nice. She felt comfortable and peaceful during the interview. Oh, and they loved her scarf. They said she looked like an air hostess. LOL. See, I told her. She'll know if she gets the job by Friday.

I can hear Sophie calling me. I'd better run off.

—G

Giselle sketched a little school building in the corner of the page and shut the cover of her journal with a soft thud. She bent over and hid it under her bed on the little ledge.

A loud knock at the door made her jump. "Come in, Soph," she said as she ran around her room searching for her other hair scrunchie. *Drats, where did I put it?*

The knock came again.

"It's unlocked. Come in, Soph," she shouted as she looked under her bed for the hair tie.

"It's not Sophie. It's your mum."

"Oh, hi, Ma," she said. She hit her head on the way up from under her bed.

"Ow." she moaned as she rubbed the sore part.

"Darling, what are you doing?" her mum asked with a confused look on her face.

"Looking for a scrunchie, but I can't find it." Giselle moaned.

"You mean that one?" Her mum pointed to the centre of Giselle's bed.

"Oh yeah." Giselle gave a little nervous laugh. She had not even seen her hair tie there.

"Okay, honey, you need to relax." Her mum grabbed her by the shoulders. "I came to say our dedication prayer with you."

Giselle nodded. At the beginning of every school term, her mum prayed with her in her room and dedicated her to God. Giselle loved this dedication prayer so much. It made her feel at peace and like God was right next to her. Nonno had done the same thing with all her aunts and uncles when they were young, and now they all did it with their kids.

Her mum took her by the hands and began to pray.

Giselle closed her eyes and began to feel at peace as her mum washed beautiful Bible verses and inspiring words over her.

When she finished praying, her mum gave her a big hug and handed her the little yellow daisy brooch. "Your father gave this to me when we met in Amsterdam so many years ago. I want you to have it as you start year eleven."

"Are you sure?" Giselle grabbed the tiny brooch and turned it over. It was her mum's favourite flower. "It's so pretty."

"Your father loved you beyond words." Her mum's eyes filled with tears, and her voice broke. "He would want you to have it. He always wanted the very best for you."

Giselle pinned the brooch on her school tie that was worn around her neck. She felt her eyes get wet. "Thanks, Mum," she said softly and leaned to hug her.

It was 7:30 a.m. by the time the cousins sat down at Kim's Deli Café. After hugs, kisses, and squeals, the girls sat at their usual spot waiting for a waiter to take their order. When that was done, they continued talking until the food started to arrive.

Giselle tried not to turn around to see if the cute surfer guy was working that morning. She hoped he was there, but maybe it was better if he wasn't, she reasoned. Her cousins' voices drifted away as she gave in to her feelings and turned around to search for him. The sound of a glass breaking made her jump out of her skin.

She refocused on her cousins and entered in the middle of their conversation. Esmeralda, called Ezi for short by her closest friends and family, was talking.

"Em, where do you get all this gossip from?" Ezi asked as she flicked her crazy curls and pushed her empty plate away from her.

"What do you mean gossip?" Em said as she took a sip of her mango smoothie. "It's news because it is informative."

Ezi fiddled with her long red shimmering fingernails. Obviously freshly done. She could gouge someone's eyes out with those. Giselle shuddered at the thought.

"Gossip, news, info . . . whatever." Ezi rolled her eyes and smoothed an invisible wrinkle from her blouse. "It's creepy that you're always up to date with everything, and you even know stuff about people at *my* school!"

"Hey, don't blame me. It's the girls on the field who gossip all the time. I just happen to be there listening." Emily grinned and took a bite from her last remaining trio of hash browns. "And it's your *ex*-school. You're a university student this year. And just a side note, that particular university had a small scandal involving two teachers having an affair last year. Did you know that?"

Gasps and laughter echoed from the cousins, except Giselle who felt her blood drain from her face at the mention of an affair. She hoped Emily didn't find out about their Nonno's affair.

Ezi laughed. "Em, you should be a reporter or journalist. You really do know everyone's gossip!""

"By the way, how are your subjects at university going??" Kiki asked as she grabbed another slice of melon and took a huge bite. Sweet juiciness dripped down her arms and elbows, and tiny drops fell onto her uniform skirt. "I'm such a dope!" She jumped off her chair and ran to the counter to get a pile of serviettes.

"Yeah." Sophie said, turning to Ezi. "I thought you hated that you're doing law.

Ezi gave an exaggerated sigh and crossed her leg on top of the other. "I want to do music but Mum wants me to be a Lawyer. I have learned not to argue with a half-Italian woman!"

"What does Uncle Alex think?" Giselle crossed her long legs trying to imitate her very cool cousin.

"Surprisingly, Dad is completely on her side," she said as she played with the ends of her curls, "but he said that if I study law first, I can switch to something else later."

"Does Aunty Miriam know that?" Silver leaned forward, a few red tresses escaping her long ponytail.

Ezi laughed. "No way, not yet. But Dad can fight it out with her. I am not crazy enough to get involved in that war zone! Puerto Rico and Italy can fight it out themselves."

"Smart," Emily said before stuffing her mouth with the last bit of her croissant. Kiki covered her mouth to smile and not drop the piece of melon from her mouth. Sophie and Silver giggled and nodded in agreement.

"Speaking of war zone," Kiki said as she took out a scented wipe to clean her sticky hands. "We'd better head to school."

"Wait!" Giselle burst out. "I have some news of my own."

Emily quickly sank back down on the chair and leaned in. "Uh, do tell. I knew this gathering would be informative."

"It's not gossip, Emily, but my mum can't find out." Giselle looked at Sophie who nodded in agreement.

"Well, what is it?" Ezi tapped her nails with impatience.

Giselle glared, ignoring her cousin's impatience, and began, "Okay, I want to go to Europe, and I need money. So, I'm getting a job here. But mum doesn't know because

she's totally against it and will kill me if she finds out."
Giselle stopped to catch her breath.

Her cousins' eyes widened and even more when
Sophie added, "There's also a guy who is totally crushing
on her. He told her so." She flicked her lovely hair to one
side and grinned like a Cheshire cat.

Giselle's eyes narrowed. "Soph!" She put her bag back
down. There was no way she was getting away now. Her
cousins would grill her for every detail.

Giselle spilled the whole story about her mum's anger
and finished with the cute surfer guy she'd met here a few
days ago. "And, no, he isn't here today." She pointed to
Emily and Esmeralda. "I know that's what you two were
going to ask," she said.

Emily and Esmeralda burst out laughing and high
fived. "You know us too well." Ezi grabbed her bag and
stood up. "I better head off you guys. Silv, I'll drop you
off, and then I'll go to my official first day of uni." She
pointed at Giselle and said, "You keep me posted about
this guy thing."

Giselle laughed. "Trust me, you'll hear all about it."

The cousins stood up and hugged each other goodbye.
Giselle watched the girls give Sophie an extra-long hug;
Silver even had tears.

Giselle looked away. She hated when Sophie went
back to boarding school. Tomorrow's goodbye would be
so hard.

Kiki handed Silver a tissue and hugged her. "Oh, Silv,
you're such a sweetheart."

Silver giggled. "I'm such a baby." She wiped her eyes.

Giselle hugged her younger cousin too. She knew the real reason Silver was crying. Her family had left the day before as well, and this was like reliving it all over again.

Giselle's heart ached. How she wished she could make things better for Silver and have her family come back home.

"Okay, Kiki, Gi, let's go." Emily pushed the door open for them to walk through, a to-go bag in one hand and a caramel bliss ball between her fingers.

"How are you getting home?" Kiki asked Sophie.

"Daddy," she said. "He dropped us off and will be in town for a little longer. He's helping me buy some things for school. I'll just text him."

"See you at home tonight," Giselle said to Sophie and waved goodbye.

"Oh, I wish I was going to school with you guys," Silver said as she followed behind. "I don't have Ezi with me anymore. At least you three have each other." She moaned.

"You should so move," Emily said. "You're just starting year ten, so no big deal."

"I can't move," Silver said flatly. "Mum and Dad are paying big bucks for me to go to Lords Hill College. I asked Mum before she left, but she says the education there is better than public school."

"Hmph." Kiki turned her face away, resenting that remark about her own school.

Giselle's head shot up; that was so unlike Kiki. She snickered.

"I think our families can be super snobby," Kiki said. "I mean, Mum wanted us to go to Crest Pointe Academy when we finished primary school, but we refused. No way."

"Except Nic." Emily rolled her eyes and shook her head at the mention of her older brother. "He practically begged Mum to send him."

Giselle laughed. Nicholas, the oldest cousin, was nice but serious. He now lived away at college, and she didn't see him much.

Kiki looked at her watch and gasped. "You guys, we need to go or we'll be late."

Emily looked at her watch and agreed they had to fly.

"Just don't kill us on the road," Kiki said to her sister as they climbed into the car.

Giselle said a quick prayer, and they were on their way.

Her stomach tightened as she saw her school come into view. *Hello, year 11,* she said to herself as they drove inside the big blue gates of Charlotte Bay High.

Chapter 8

After wishing her cousins a good day, Giselle darted to the art block area to meet up with her friends, Quinn and Indigo. She spotted them a mile away, and when they looked up and saw her, they squealed and ran to hug her.

"Hey girls, do you mind?!" a voice yelled.

"Yeah, we're trying to play a game," another voice echoed.

Giselle disentangled herself from her friends as they finally became aware of their surroundings.

Giselle covered her mouth. "Oops. Sorry, guys," she said as she moved away from the basketball court under the hoop.

Quinn lifted her arm and shouted. "Sorry, dudes. We didn't realise we were on the court."

The girls looked at each other and laughed.

"Hey, don't I get a hug?" Giselle spun around at the male voice and grinned. "Oh, Joshy. Hi." She hugged her cousin, the twins' triplet.

Josh wiggled his eyebrows up and down. "So . . . I hear there's a guy in the picture for you?"

Giselle gaped "What? Already?" She grabbed his arm and stepped away from her friends. "Who told you that? Never mind. It was Emily, wasn't it?" Giselle sighed.

Josh grinned and nodded, his grey-blue eyes dancing with mischief. Giselle couldn't get angry at him. He was the sweetest. Just as she opened her mouth to speak, the bell rang announcing that the first day of school was now official.

"Yikes, the bell!" Giselle squeaked. "Good luck, Joshy, hope year twelve is good." She gave him one more hug.

"You too, Gi. Hope your year is cool!" He winked and jogged towards his friends.

Giselle grinned as some girls nearby watched him with an adoring look. Giselle shook her head. Josh was oblivious that the girls at school found him irresistible.

She joined her friends. Quinn stared at her with an arm on one hip and her eyebrows raised. Indi had her arms crossed over her chest, although her eyes also lingered on Josh a little longer. Giselle hid a smile.

"There's a *guy*? We heard Josh ask about a guy. Why didn't you tell us?" A how-dare-you-not-tell-us tone escaped Indigo's lips.

Quinn lifted her hand in the air as if to stop traffic. "Not another step until you tell us the whole thing," she demanded.

Giselle grimaced. "It wasn't on purpose, you guys. Seriously, this happened like two days ago. I'll tell you everything at lunch, I promise."

Her friends looked at each other and smiled. "Good," Indigo said.

They moved to room 23 where the year 11 students met for roll call.

"By the way, Indi, your hair turned out great!" Giselle said as she touched her friend's jet-black hair. "Makes your eyes pop."

Quinn nodded. "I totally agree. They're like azure."

"Uh, yeah they are!" Giselle leaned close to her friend's face and stared at her eyes.

Indigo stepped back and made a funny face. "What are you two talking about? And what is azure?"

"It's a gorgeous blue we use in our paintings," Giselle explained, grinning widely. "It will capture the love of your life."

"A colour that Josh would definitely love," Quinn teased.

Indigo scoffed, "You two are nuts. Let's hurry to roll call."

The girls laughed all the way to roll call, but they became serious when the deputy principal stood in front of the class waiting for them to arrive.

Giselle twisted her mouth to one side and said in a whisper, "Feels official."

Year 11 had truly begun.

Dear Diary,

I'm dying! We've already been given our assignment and exam timetable for this term, and it's huge. I pretty much have an assignment for every single subject. All the assignments seem to be due the same week. I don't know how I will keep up with school and work. If I get the job at Kim's Deli Café.

For art, we're studying Van Gogh and need to do a big self-portrait, but Mrs. Reed said our portrait can't be just an ordinary portrait—she wants it to have a meaning that represents our life. I have made a start but keep getting stuck. I have no ideas or inspiration. How am I supposed to make it extraordinary? Maybe I'm just stressed because I'm also going to have to fit in work.

Maybe Mum is right, and I should concentrate on school only. But how am I going to save if I'm not working? Mum doesn't even make much anyways. I know I can do it! I just need to get organised ASAP.

Oh, and I met up with Rachel today after school. We were going to meet at the library, but seriously, she has three boys, and they would not be quiet in a library. So, we met near my bus stop at the Freeze Yo. It's her kids' favourite yogurt and ice cream place to hang out after school. She's so amazing, and I felt super bad lying to her that mum knows about the job.

I hope my interview goes well tomorrow—I feel sick just thinking about it. I wonder if I'll see that guy. I hope so! Okay, I'd better pen off and get out of romance land. I have a cousin who I need to spend time with!

—G

Giselle sketched a love heart at the bottom of the page, closed her book with a thump, and lay on her back to reflect on her day. She was supposed to be working on her assignment, but she was not motivated. Outside her door, she could hear rushed footsteps going back and forth. Her heart turned. It was Sophie and Uncle Mick packing and getting her things ready. He was driving her to school early in the morning. Giselle sighed. She was going to miss her cousin so much. Why couldn't Soph go to school with her instead?

Giselle remembered when they were both around eight and lived at Nonno and Grandmama's house. Uncle Mick travelled all the time and was barely home, so he couldn't look after Sophie. Giselle had loved having her there, and they had become pretty much like sisters. Then one day, when they were twelve, Soph was over at her Dad's house for the weekend, and she called Giselle sobbing. Between tears, Sophie told her that Uncle Mick was sending her away to boarding school three hours away!

Giselle was furious and didn't want to talk to Uncle Mick ever again for being so mean. But her mum had taken her out to eat and explained that Uncle Mick was grieving and was doing what he thought was best for Soph. Through tears, Giselle nodded and promised to forgive him.

Giselle smiled weakly as the thoughts poured out. That memory felt like hundreds of years ago instead of four.

Reluctantly, Giselle got out of bed, hiding her journal as always, and went to help her cousin pack her bags.

Giselle plopped onto Sophie's cream and pink velvet bed, folded her legs under her, and straightened her patchwork-print cotton pants, a gift from Sophie.

Sophie followed suit. "I don't want to go, Gi." Her eyes welled with tears. "I'm finding it harder and harder to go back."

Giselle opened her mouth to tell Sophie she felt the same, but she knew she had to encourage her, so instead she pasted a smile and determined to lift up her cousin's spirits. "Soph, you will be fine. Only two years left there, and then we can travel Europe together and maybe even go to the same uni or college or wherever we want." Giselle grinned. "We will be unstoppable."

Sophie rolled her eyes and wiped a falling tear. "Okay. Yeah, we will be unstoppable. The Hayes sisters' superpower."

Giselle burst out laughing. "We haven't called each other the Hayes sisters since you left to boarding school. Wow, it's been ages."

Sophie nodded. "We *are* pretty much sisters. We are the only cousins with the same last name. Well, you have your dad's too, but still . . ." Her voice trailed off as she picked an invisible thread on her silk pants. "We also each only have one parent." She whispered the last word.

Giselle nodded and added, "And your dad and my mum are twins. So that makes us sisters forever!" By now, both of them had tears spilling down their cheeks.

"Yeah, that's true," Sophie said, her lips lifting in the corners. "Anyways, let's not ruin tonight, okay? No more tears."

"Deal!" Giselle said, extending her little pinkie. "Pinkie promise."

"Pinkie promise." Giselle hooked fingers with Sophie's and laughed. It felt like they were eight again making promises to be forever friends and sisters.

A knock at the door interrupted their tears and chuckles. Giselle watched as Sophie jumped out of bed and hurried to open her bedroom door. A gasp and a shout escaped her lips. Giselle's eyes widened as Sophie opened the door wide and her cousins shouted, "Surprise!"

Their cousins paraded in with pizza boxes, popcorn, and drinks. Sophie turned to look at Giselle and clapped her hands. "You guys! What a shock." She ran to hug each one as they trailed in.

Giselle hopped out of bed and giggled. This was such fun.

"We couldn't let you go without having a cousin farewell and, of course, lots of food," Emily said as she set a pizza box on Sophie's study desk.

Esmeralda tossed her wild curls to one side and said, "I mean, we know it's a school night, but when will you be back, Soph? Not for three months, so we had to come party."

"And . . . ," Silver announced holding up a paper bag in her hand, "we brought your favourite."

"Caramel Tim Tams!" Kiki announced as she grabbed the shopping bag from Silver and took out the packaged dessert.

Giselle laughed at Sophie's reaction as she took the Tim Tams and clutched them to her chest. "You guys know me too well! Thank you so much . . . and thank you for coming. You made my night. No, you made my year!"

"Girls." Giselle spun around at her mum's voice. "The rumpus room is ready for you to eat. I've put out paper plates and cups and serviettes. Go enjoy."

"Thanks, Aunt Lusi," the girls said in chorus.

"Ma, did you know about this plan?" Giselle asked.

Her mum laughed. "Naturally!"

Giselle rolled her eyes and laughed too.

As everyone headed downstairs, Giselle smiled. She loved her cousins, and yes, sometimes they argued, especially with Ezi who complained about everything and was as headstrong as a bull. Still, she loved them and loved them even more for spending time with Sophie before she left. This was going to be a great night and probably a late one too.

Chapter 9

The squawks and screeches of the birds above made
Giselle jump. She stared at the sky as dark menacing
clouds grouped together in the middle of the sky. A
sudden spark of lightning streaked the sky, and a rumble
of thunder followed. Giselle gulped. A storm brewed
in the horizon. The wind picked up, and suddenly the
trees howled. Panic seized her heart, and she struggled
to get out of her seat. She pulled again. She was stuck.
Something or someone was holding her down. Giselle
looked down at her belly. She was strapped with a seat
belt securely around her waist. Laughter echoed around
her, and then, with a big whoosh, she felt herself fly to the
heavens. Giselle screamed as another round of thunder
boomed, then covered her eyes so she would not see
herself touch the lightning.

"Make it stop!" she yelled. "Stop." Her shrieks echoed
in the darkening afternoon. More thunder roared.

"Don't panic, sweetheart. Daddy just wants you to fly
higher." At the sound of a male voice, Giselle turned her

head on her seat and saw her dad. His kind eyes crinkled behind his glasses as he beamed at her.

"Daddy." Her voice squeaked like a mouse. "The storm," she whispered and pointed at the danger approaching.

"You are safe with me, no need to panic," he said soothingly.

She shook her head vigorously. She wasn't safe. A big storm was coming.

She wriggled in her seat to get away. She pulled, but she went nowhere.

Trapped.

Suddenly strange female hands with long fingers appeared out of nowhere and reached for her. Giselle gasped for air and kicked her legs violently. "Don't touch me! Don't touch me!" she yelled.

The woman leaned close, and a little smile played on her lips. Then out of nowhere her face morphed into Nonno's face. Giselle shrieked as a crack of thunder vibrated and shook her swing.

Giselle sat up on her bed screaming. Her breathing came in heavy breaths, her chest heaved, and her hands trembled. Outside, soft rain pelted on her window and roof, and a sudden light illuminated the room. She hunched over and covered her head with her summer blanket.

"Go away," she whispered to the thunder. She sent a quick prayer and asked God to help her. The sound of thunder came from a distance, and Giselle exhaled.

A soft knock on her door startled her. Shaken, she waited.

"Giselle, honey, can I come in?"

At the sound of her mum's voice Giselle let out a little cry of relief and called out, "Yes."

She reached for her lamp, and light bathed the room. The soft glow and her mother's presence quieted her heart.

"Ma," she whispered as she stretched out her hand.

Her mum squeezed it gently and sat on her bed. "I thought I'd check on you," she said with a wink.

Giselle attempted a smile and leaned her head into her mum's shoulder. "Mum, I feel so dumb to be so afraid of a storm. I'm old and shouldn't feel scared. I mean, can you imagine what my friends would think if they knew?" Giselle covered her face with her hands.

"Oh, honey, don't worry about them." Her mum grabbed her hand. "And you're not old at all!"

"Why do you think I hate storms so much? When did it start?" Giselle moaned.

Her mum cleared her throat. "You were around three years old. It was right after your dad's funeral, and you were alone in the living room." Her mum's eyes glistened. "I was in the kitchen making you something to eat, and suddenly you screamed." She paused for a moment. "I rushed to see what had happened, and you were huddled with a cushion in the corner of the room, screaming and crying. Telling something to go away."

"How did you know it was the storm?"

"Well, I held you in my arms and asked what was wrong. You pointed outside to the rain and then an ear-splitting clap of thunder rolled and you screamed again, telling it to go away."

"Why was I scared then and not before?" Giselle frowned. "Was it because of Dad?"

Her mum shrugged. "Probably. Trauma affects us all in different ways."

Giselle nodded and listened as thunder boomed in the distance. She closed her eyes and leaned closer into her mum.

"Ma, I think I need therapy or something. I don't like this at all," she muttered.

Her mother nodded and patted her hand. "Go to sleep, honey. You have school tomorrow. I will stay here for a bit."

Giselle nodded, then closed her eyes.

You're such a baby, she told herself as she thought about the nightmare and the storm. She couldn't tell her mum about the nightmare. What would she think if she knew?

Giselle shook her head and soon fell into an uneasy sleep.

Early the next morning, Giselle and her mum stood outside saying goodbye to Sophie and Uncle Mick.

"Missing you already!" Giselle shouted as Uncle Mick's car drove down the driveway of the house. Sophie's body stuck halfway out the window as she waved frantically and blew kisses.

"Missing you more, Gi," she shouted. "And missing you, Aunt Lusi."

Giselle and her mum watched the car drive off. Uncle Mick stuck his hand outside the window and waved goodbye. Sophie blew one last kiss and vanished back into the car.

With a big sigh, Giselle leaned her head onto her mum's shoulder and watched them drive out of the ornate iron gates.

"I wish it was the holidays already," she said and dried a little tear from the corner of her eye.

Her mum touched her side plait and smiled. "It'll go faster than you think, honey. Hang in there."

Giselle nodded and followed her mum inside. She shuddered as they walked back inside; the mansion had begun to feel gloomy and hollow.

"Go get ready for school," her mum instructed as Giselle moved towards the kitchen and her mother headed upstairs.

"Yes, Ma. I'm just going to get my lunchbox ready." Giselle opened the creamy marbled cupboards and grabbed her rice crackers, vegan cheese, and salad sprigs. She packed fruits, water, nuts, a mint herbal tea, then closed her lunch pack.

When she got to her room, she spotted a rectangular-shaped box with a cute pink ribbon decorating the top. It sat next to her school uniform on top of her bed.

Curious, Giselle unwrapped the box, and her breath caught. There in the box was the most beautiful pair of sandals she'd ever owned. The tan straps were decorated with a thin gold band, turquoise gem flowers, and petite diamante leaves.

Giselle hugged them to her heart and pulled out the note.

"To my Hayes sister, enjoy these!

Love Sophie

PS: Wear them and don't say they're too pretty to wear. I want to see them totally worn-out next time I see you. Xo"

Giselle laughed, tried them on and was mesmerized. It was like they had been made just for her. She grabbed her phone and sent Sophie a quick text.

LOVE THEM, SOPH. THANK YOU! XX

YOU'RE WELCOME! XXOO

"Honey, are you ready?" her mum called out across the house.

"Almost!" She put the sandals back into the box, set her phone down on her bed, and made a mad dash to get dressed.

As she headed out the door, she remembered she had the job interview with Kim that afternoon.

"Oops." She ran back in and packed a pair of flats and a black-and-white dress Grandmama had given her one Christmas. Giselle folded the dress neatly and added a body spritz. Satisfied, she said bye to her mum and went out the door to the bus stop.

Art class came too soon for Giselle that day. She didn't feel ready to face her assignment. Or her teacher. She was supposed to have nicely drawn ideas but all she had to show were incomplete messy sketches.

Giselle leaned over to Quinn and gasped, "Oh, wow! That's turning out gorgeous," she exclaimed as she admired her friend's self-portrait.

Quinn smiled. "Aw thanks, Gi. What have you done so far?" Quinn tucked a strand of her messy short brown hair behind her ear.

Giselle clutched her A3 art journal to her chest and said, "You can't look. It's a surprise."

Quinn laughed. "Okay, okay." She went back to her drawing.

Giselle bit her bottom lip and looked around the classroom. It looked like everyone was busy drawing. Even Joel, the class clown and notorious lazybones, had his head down drawing his self-portrait. Giselle glanced out the window and heaved a sigh. In the distance, she could see Emily and Josh in their PE class running around. Usually, sports felt too strenuous for Giselle, but today she would rather be out there instead of sitting and staring at her incomplete and uninspired sketches.

"Giselle?" The voice of her teacher interrupted her thoughts.

Giselle turned and gave her a half-hearted smile. "Yes, Miss?"

Mrs. Reed moved her dark fringed hair out of her eyes. "I've noticed that you haven't been drawing. This class started thirty minutes ago, and each time I look your way, you looked pained. Is everything okay?"

Giselle plopped her art journal with a loud thud onto the table and sighed, "I have zero, zilch inspiration. I don't know what to do."

Her teacher frowned as she fixed her chunky turquoise earring and said, "Have you started with your brainstorming map?"

Giselle nodded and opened her book to show her.

"You've got some great ideas here, so what is stopping you from creating?" Mrs. Reed moved the book closer to her and studied the ideas.

Giselle shrugged. "I think what's throwing me off is that the assignment says it has to be a portrait with a difference or something like that. So, I'm stuck."

Her teacher nodded, her bright earrings bouncing from side to side. "Okay, how about you come to see me tomorrow during lunchtime, and let's see if we can break down the assignment into little parts. You are a great artist, Giselle. Don't underestimate yourself."

"Thanks, Mrs. Reed." Giselle closed her book.

"In the meantime, could you draw yourself in the middle of the page, a rough sketch, and then I would like you to write around the image all the things you like. Everything from colour to food and clothes, et cetera."

Giselle nodded; she could do that.

She opened her book again and began drawing. She was so intrigued in her work that she didn't hear the bell ring telling her it was time to go home.

"Coming, Gi?" Quinn said as she packed her artwork.

Giselle looked up at the clock. "What? Already?"

Quinn laughed. "Yeah, the bell rang. We can go home now, you know."

Giselle rolled her eyes. "I didn't hear it." She giggled but suddenly stopped. "Oh my goodness! I just remembered."

"What?" Quinn frowned.

"I have the job interview today! Ah, I'm scared." Giselle tapped her fingers on the desk then turned to look at the clock again. "Okay, I have thirty minutes to change and get to Kim's. Yikes."

"Don't stress. You'll be awesome. Plus, you know their menu back to front. That's a bonus."

Giselle swallowed and nodded. "Okay, I'd better go. I don't want to be late. See you tomorrow!"

"Text me!" Quinn shouted after her.

Giselle waved and ran all the way to her locker. She was surprised to see Kiki and Emily waiting for her.

"Is everything okay?" she asked as she opened her locker door and took out her bag with her clothes in it.

"Of course," they said in unison and smiled directly at her.

"We're going to take you to the café so you're not late," Kiki explained.

"You can't catch the bus today, and we have no after-school commitments, so we can take you. Plus, when you get the job, you can bring me leftover deliciousness." Emily smiled and hoisted her long chocolate-brown hair into a bun.

"Aw, you guys," Giselle gushed. "Thank you!" She grabbed her clothes, her bag, and slammed the locker door shut.

"By the way, do you think that cute guy will be there?" Emily grinned and raised her eyebrows.

"Em, don't make her nervous!" Kiki hit her sister on the arm.

Giselle moaned. "I hope not! I'm so nervous as it is. I hope I don't see him at all today."

"You won't," Kiki said. "It's probably his day off or something."

Giselle nodded and suddenly felt her stomach drop. What would she do if she did see him?

She shook her head; she didn't have time to think about him today. She needed to calm herself and hope for the best. She smiled at the twins and hurried to get changed. At least now she wasn't going to be late.

Chapter 10

Giselle waved goodbye to the twins and inhaled deeply as they drove off. Truth be told, she felt bad feeling this way, but she was glad Emily couldn't get out with her. There had been no parking, so they could only drop her off at the front. Giselle was nervous as it was and didn't want Emily adding more nervous energy, especially if she saw the cute surfer guy.

The little bell above the door jingled overhead, and all of a sudden, she spotted him cleaning a table. Her heart lurched and tightened.

What could she do? Could she turn around and hide somewhere? Maybe if she walked really fast to the counter, he wouldn't spot her. Or she could pretend she was reading her resume and walk by quickly.

Hoping to go undetected, she tightened the grip on her bag and rushed towards the counter.

"Hey!" a male voice said, interrupting her invisibility.

Giselle stopped and closed her eyes before slowly turning around. Just by the sound of his voice, she knew he was grinning.

"Oh hi." She forced a smile. *Gee, how could he be cuter than the last time?* she wondered. Her stomach did a crazy somersault as he moved closer to her.

"Good to see you again, Giselle." His face dimpled when he smiled.

Her eyes became big as saucers. "You know my name?"

He nodded. "Kim told me after you left the other night. She said you were going to be coming in for an interview."

Giselle could only nod. The sound of her name on his lips sounded musical. How had her name never sounded pretty coming out of anyone else's mouth before? She was about to speak when she was interrupted by Kim who walked through the employees-only door and motioned for her to come to the back office.

Giselle looked at the guy and pursed her lips. He smiled and leaned in close to her. "You will be amazing," he whispered, then winked and gently squeezed her arm.

Her knees turned to mush, and she couldn't breathe. Her arm burned from his touch. *Hold it together!* she told herself. She managed to murmur a tiny thank-you and followed Kim for her interview.

She glanced over her shoulder and saw him still standing there watching her walk away. Giselle swallowed; She couldn't afford to let him distract her any further.

Dear Diary,

I had the interview, so I can't turn back. Kim was a real boss interviewing me. There was another girl in the interview with her. Her name's Talia, and I think she's the manager. She's kind of scary, serious, like a rock-and-roll girl. Leather jacket and black skinny jeans, boots, and her dark hair is styled in kind of long choppy layers. She looks fierce. Yikes, I don't want to be in her bad books.

Anyways, the questions were okay. I had practiced with Rachel when she signed the paper the other day, so they weren't too bad. Except I tripped over a question about what to do if someone was being rude or obnoxious. I said call the cops. LOL. They said no, that I should call the manager. Whoops. Okay, so now it's funny, but during the interview it was humiliating. I felt my face turn all shades of red and maybe even purple.

Anyways, I don't know if they'll call me or not, but I'll find out tomorrow. Aah, I'm not ready. They said I would work Tuesdays, Thursdays, and Sunday nights. Those days feel doable. It's only a three-hour shift each time. I just have to come up with an excuse to tell Mum why I'll be coming home late from school. Ugh, that's another thing that's eating my insides. I hate lying to her and I wish I could tell her. I mean, I will tell her but not yet. I will wait a week or two.

Aaaand, I saw the guy as I was leaving! I almost fainted. He waved and grinned at me from where he was taking an order. I was disappointed he couldn't come chat with me. He's sooo cute. I don't think he's in school any longer, though; he looks a little older than the guys at my school. Plus, he acts so much more mature. I really hope I get the job and get to see him more. But I honestly don't know if I can hold a job, do school, and have a boyfriend all at the same time. It feels way too much. I wonder if my mum is right after all.

Anyways, Soph called me a few times this afternoon, but I was in the interview. She said she wanted to wish me luck. She's so sweet. She's already settling at her school and decorating her room and arranging all the furniture. Uncle Mick is on his way to London (so lucky, I wish I was going). She said he was really upset about leaving her this time round. He even joked that she would do senior year back in Charlotte Bay. Soph said YES, but he told her he was just kidding. He said the school she was going to was good for her.

Okay, so I have to stop journaling and go shower. I'm exhausted. The creepy dream I keep having hasn't let me sleep properly. I hate it. I really hope I sleep tonight.

They also announced more rain and a possible storm. No!! I hate it. I have prayed to God so many times to take away my fear of storms. He hasn't so far. I don't know if He listens to my prayers.

—G

Giselle chewed the end of her black pen and stared at the corner wall thoughtfully. Did God listen to prayers? She heard He did, but He didn't seem to be listening to hers. She sighed deeply and went back to the page and finished off with a tiny sketch of Kim's Deli Café. She signed the entry, then closed the book with a thump.

A little flash of lighting danced outside her window, but there was no sound of thunder. Relieved, she rushed through her shower and got ready to do some homework.

After a few hours of homework, she stretched her sore body and decided to go to bed. Her clock said 12:15 a.m.

Giselle groaned. Year 11 was already way too busy, and it hadn't even fully begun.

Heavy rain pelted on the roof, and Giselle smiled. She loved rain. The raindrop sounds were comforting. It was the storms she didn't like.

As soon as her head hit the pillow, she fell asleep.

The rude screeching of the alarm woke Giselle up with a jolt. She sat up and looked around, her head thick and groggy. She was usually a happy morning person, but today she wished she could throw out the alarm clock and go back to sleep. She looked at the time on her clock and grunted. How would she function today on only five hours of sleep?

"Okay, I'm going to the lighthouse to get some fresh air," she said out loud. Determined, Giselle put on her fitness gear, grabbed a bag, threw her water bottle, Bible, and pencil case into it, and tiptoed to the garage to grab her bike.

The crisp early morning air made her suddenly feel alive. Summertime was a bonus, for the sun was out by 4:30 a.m., and the lovely rain from the previous night had made the morning cool and fresh. She inhaled as she took in the ocean scenery, the breeze, and the people passing by. She saw runners, cyclists, and walkers all the way to the lighthouse.

After locking her bike at the bike racks, Giselle sat at her usual spot and read her Bible. She prayed and asked

God to take the nightmares away. Her thoughts ventured into her recurring nightmare, her art assignment, and her dishonesty with her mum. Even though she felt energised after her bike ride, she also felt heavyhearted.

Feeling deflated, Giselle picked up her phone and began writing Rachel a quick text.

Hey Rachel, sorry to bother you so early. But could you pray for me, please? I'm having a really bad dream almost every second night, and I don't like it. I'm also terrified of storms. I feel like such a baby. It's humiliating. I want that to go! Please pray.

Giselle read the message about ten times, but she felt really weird telling Rachel about her nightmare and her fear of storms. In a flash she deleted the message. She would just have to battle out her issues with God. No one must know.

"Giselle!" The bellow of her mother's voice startled Giselle as she walked out of the shower. It was as if she had washed her anxiety away; she was feeling so much better than this morning. Until now.

"Ma, what's wrong?" Giselle stared at her mum who was rushing up the stairs two at a time.

"Oh, honey, I got the job!" Her mum's eyes popped and sparkled.

"Ma, that is awesome!" Giselle squealed and ran into her mother's arms. "See, I told you, you would get it."

"I know you did. You had more confidence than I did."
Her mum squeezed her hands. "I have to go in today for
an orientation and sign some paperwork."

"When do you start?" Giselle walked towards her
bedroom. Her mum linked arms with her.

"Monday at seven a.m. sharp. I'm going to be working
long days, honey. Twelve-hour shifts! I won't be home
as much. Only on the weekends—" Her mum stopped
walking. "Oh, Giselle, you need me more than ever in
your senior year. I feel like I'm abandoning you!"

Giselle shook her head. "No way. You deserve this
job, Ma. Don't worry about me. I'll be so busy studying
anyways."

"Are you sure?" Her mum tilted her head to one side
and looked at Giselle intently.

Giselle rolled her eyes. Sometimes her mum acted as
if she was three instead of sixteen. "Yes, I'm sure. You go
work and enjoy it. I'm really proud of you." She leaned in
and gave her mum a big hug.

"Thank you, honey. I'll go ring that brother of mine."
She swirled around and moved in the other direction
towards her own room. "Hopefully he's awake. Oh well,
I'll wake him if he's not."

Giselle shook her head and laughed as she watched her
mother practically glide down the hall. Then a sudden
realisation hit her. If her mum was busy every weekday,
she didn't need to know about Giselle's job. It looked like
her secret would be safe after all. She breathed a sigh of
relief.

Her phone rang as she entered her bedroom. She dashed to see if it was one of the cousins, but she didn't recognise the number.

Hesitantly, she answered, "Hello?"

"Giselle, it's Kim from the café." Giselle froze. "Hello?" the voice at the other end said.

Giselle cleared her throat. "Hi, Kim." She put on a smile so she sounded normal.

"I'm calling to congratulate you. You got the job!"

"Oh wow. Really? Wow, thank you!" Giselle's hand trembled slightly.

"Come for an orientation on Sunday, and we can sign the paperwork and take care of all the formalities. We can talk more then."

After hanging up, Giselle flopped onto her bed and hooted. *I have a job!*

How weird that she and her mum had both landed a job on the same day.

She picked up her phone and sent a quick text to Sophie. She got ready for school in record time and went without breakfast. Her stomach danced with excitement.

Chapter 11

Giselle took a deep breath as she pushed the door open of Kim's Deli Café and walked in, the bell above the door once again dinging to announce her arrival. She looked around and smiled. She had loved this place for ages, and now she would get to work here. She hoped she could do a good job. There was no way she was going to get fired. She had two years to save all the money she could for Europe. Her stomach dropped at the possibility of going to England, Italy, and Paris. Finally, she would be where her dad had been and visit his grave. Giselle beamed as she hurried to the counter to ask for Kim.

After Kim went over the rules, she gave Giselle an employee's handbook, an apron, and a black T-shirt with the Kim's Deli Café logo embroidered on the top right-hand corner. After her orientation was over, Giselle placed everything into her oversize tote bag and headed out the door. She walked outside to her mint-coloured bike. She patted her bag carefully. Guilt washed over her. What if her mum found out? The ringing of her phone made her jump, and she inhaled sharply when she saw her mum's name pop up. *Oh no*, she thought, *she found out! She's going to kill me.*

"Hey, Mum." She forced her voice to sound cheery.

"Honey, where are you? I didn't realise you were going out today?" her mother said.

"Um, yeah. I'm . . . I just needed to check some things out in the bookstore," she lied.

"Oh, okay." Her mum paused briefly before speaking again. "I'm going out with my sisters to celebrate my new job. Do you want me to leave food ready for you?"

"No, Ma. I'll buy something and take it home." She sighed with relief. "Thank you, though. Go have fun!"

Her mum blew a loud kiss over the phone and hung up.

Giselle decided to ride her bike near the water where they had the best sushi in town. Mr. and Mrs. Chow were lovely and always gave her the fattest, freshest vegetarian sushi they had.

Just as she rounded the corner to the Chows' eatery, she almost crashed into a pedestrian coming out of the parking lot. "Oops, sorry, I wasn't looking," she explained as she looked up. Her words froze midsentence, and suddenly she couldn't breathe. The café guy!

A huge grin appeared on his face when he recognised her. "Giselle!" He held onto a helmet and stared at her face.

Giselle's mouth became dry. She hopped off her bike, licked her lips and stammered, "Um, hi, you . . . looks like you ride a motorbike?"

He glanced down at his black helmet and laughed. "Yeah, I have a motorbike. Not that my mum likes it, but it gets me around to places and it's cheaper to keep than a car."

Giselle nodded. "My mum would kill me if I got on a bike!" she exclaimed.

"So, I heard you got the job at Kim's—congrats." His cheeks dimpled.

"Thanks. I'm really nervous." She was extra nervous because he would be there too.

"Don't be. You'll be fine. And I can help you if you get stuck. Just ask me anything." His green eyes sparkled.

Giselle could drown in those eyes. *Get a grip*, she told herself and moved slightly back a few steps to put some distance between them.

"When do you start?" he asked her.

"Tuesday is my first shift," she said. "Do you work every day?"

He nodded, and his shaggy sandy-blond hair shifted over his eyes.

Giselle wondered how his hair would feel if she touched it. Her eyes travelled to his face and paused at his lips. How would it feel to kiss him? She gasped. What was wrong with her? She felt mortified she was having these thoughts. She needed to leave and fast.

"I better let you go," she said quickly. "See you Tuesday."

"By the way, my name's Jace." He extended out his hand and smiled. "Nice to finally meet you properly, Giselle."

As if in slow motion, she lifted her hand and shook his. Her stomach flipped, and her breath caught.

"Nice to meet you too," she managed to say. "I've got to go." She motioned with her hand, and after a brief bye she hurried down the path towards home.

It wasn't until she arrived that she remembered that she had forgotten her sushi. She felt so dumb and silly for letting a guy control her emotions like that.

"God, I need help," she whispered.

Back at Uncle Mick's house, she managed to find a few bread rolls in the fridge, a slice of tofu, and some salad mix. She made herself a sandwich and headed to her room to eat. She didn't want to be downstairs. The empty, silent house saddened her spirit.

After she devoured her sandwich, she decided to go to the lighthouse. She would take her art journal and work on her assignment there. She was sure something might inspire her. Besides, it was a great excuse to leave the eerie house for a few hours.

Dear Diary,

I'm such a dope! I mean, seriously, I have been thinking about Jace all afternoon. I got to the lighthouse and was supposed to be drawing a self-portrait and guess what? I ended up drawing him! Argh, why! Talking to my art teacher the other day at lunchtime kind of helped, but I'm still stuck. I don't even know why.

Anyways, back to Jace. Why did he have to appear now when I'm in year 11—seriously?

While I was at the lighthouse drawing Jace (his name is nice, by the way, suits him perfectly! LOL), I had a brilliant idea. For my art assignment, I'm supposed to draw a self-portrait "with a difference," so I'm thinking of going to Grandma's house and checking out the albums she has stashed in the family room. I mean, she has them all dated and with names. Talk about organised (or pedantic, as Mum calls it). You know, Mum and Grandmama had issues before. Grandmama was totally opposed to Mum gallivanting (as Grandmama called it) across Europe. She wanted her to stay home after she finished uni. But hey, hold on a sec. I just realised something: Mum is opposed to me travelling around Europe! How odd that she is being Grandma now. I think I'll tell her that next time she tells me I can't go. She will get mad and hate it because she does not want to be like Grandmama at all. She's more like Nonno, a bit of a free spirit, adventurous.

I think this week after school I'm going to catch the bus to her house and check out the albums. I know I will be totally inspired by old photos. Now I'm beginning to get excited. I might be able to get some really cool things. I've looked around at our albums at our house, and Mum has only one tiny one, with photos of me when I was like two years old. It's of no use. Anyways, it's getting late, and I bet Mum will be home soon. I had to leave the lighthouse before it got dark. Mum would kill me if I stayed out there late. Besides, I'm freaked out when it gets dark and I'm all alone at the lighthouse.

Yep, spot on, I was right. I can hear the door opening downstairs.

It must be Mum coming back from her sisters' date. Uncle Mick isn't home for a few more days, so it can't be him. All right, I better go see what she has for me. She usually brings dessert back and it might be something I love with mint. Yum!

—G

81

Giselle drew a mint macaron cookie in the corner of the page, closed her book, and hurried downstairs.

She heard the sound of dishes clinking and the fridge door opening then closing.

"Hey, Ma." Giselle's bare feet barely made a sound on the frosty marble floor of the kitchen.

"Hey, honey, how was your day?" Her mum popped her head around from behind the fridge door.

Giselle looked around. It looked like her mum had been shopping: brown paper bags were displayed across the kitchen bench. One was labelled Veggie Green Hut. Giselle gasped and looked inside the bag. "Ma, you never buy at this deli; it's too expensive. Uh, yum." Inside she saw a marinated tofu pack, pistachio nuts, gourmet cream cheese, water crackers sprinkled with wasabi, and a tub of mango yoghurt.

Her mother laughed. "I am now a working woman with a secure full-time job, so I wanted to splurge and celebrate." Giselle took the ingredients out of the bags and placed them on the bench while her mum put them away.

"But you don't eat any of these things," Giselle said.

Her mother paused in front of the cold fridge and turned to her. "I know, honey. These are for you. Our tastes are completely opposite, but I just decided to buy your favourite foods." Her mum smiled and went back to putting the goodies in the fridge.

Giselle's gasped, and she ran to her mum and gave her a hug. "Aw, Ma, that is the sweetest thing ever. Thank you!!" She planted a big, loud kiss on her cheek.

Her mother laughed, closed the refrigerator door, and turned to Giselle. "You are a wonderful daughter. Have I ever told you that?"

Giselle's heart melted.

"When all my sisters and Mick were trying to get me behind the wheel of a car again, you stood up for me and told them to leave me alone. You always defend me and care for me. You know how scatterbrained I can be. Sometimes I feel you're my mum!" Her mother giggled and laced her arm with Giselle's.

"Ma, you're my mum, and I will always defend you and love you. Besides, I was mad they were forcing you to drive again. I mean, after the accident there is no way you would have driven again. So dumb." Giselle shook her long brown hair, a few strands falling over her eyes and cheeks.

Her mum shuddered when Giselle mentioned the accident. She didn't like to talk about it, and Giselle barely ever mentioned it. A few years back she had asked how it happened, and her mum had burst into tears. Giselle had never asked again. She knew her dad had died from that crash, but she didn't know all the details.

"Oh, by the way, I bought us dessert! Want to sit outside on the veranda, watch the yachts, and indulge?" Her mother lifted her eyebrows and headed to the freezer.

Giselle knew the accident conversation was over.

"Yes, please." Her eyes widened as her mum brought out two tubs of gourmet ice creams. "Mum, you really did splurge!" Her laugh echoed in the enormous house as she hurried to grab two ice cream bowls and some caramel and chocolate sauce.

Giselle loved ending the day on a positive note, but a tiny twinge of guilt washed over her heart as she remembered her secret job. She hoped her mum wouldn't find out for a long time to come.

Chapter 12

The soft, silvery laughter and joyous moment popped like a burst balloon as a clad of thunder reverberated around her. Giselle screamed and covered her ears. Soft rain had started to drizzle on her head and arms, but for some reason they felt painful. Above her head birds were screeching as they headed south, away from the rain and the storm. Even *they* were panicked. Strong wind had begun to pick up, and the rain increased.

Giselle wriggled like a worm but was trapped. The safety belt of the swing secured her in place. The loud bang of another round of thunder shook her, and she shrieked again. "Take me out! Take me out!" she yelled.

Suddenly her father's face appeared, and his grin changed to concern. "Sweetheart, it's okay. It's okay. Daddy is here. You are safe."

His strong, manly hands reached for her, but they were swiftly replaced by a woman's hands. Strong, slim hands reached for Giselle, who pushed back against her swing to get away. But escape was impossible. She was confined to the swing. The hands reached and grabbed her by the waist.

Giselle screamed and burst into tears. In her anxiety she reached for the hands and scratched them. In pain, the feminine hands pulled back.

Giselle woke up with a jerk. Her heart pounded violently in her chest. Her breaths came short and fast.

She turned on her lamp and sat up. "God, why am I having these nightmares?"

Then she realized: she'd been having them ever since she found out her Nonno had had an affair—at least she assumed he had.

Slowly, Giselle got out of bed and went to get the pouch with the locket in it. She opened it and admired the details again. She touched the embossed letters—O. A. B. What did they mean?

Her Nonno's words the last time she had seen him alive haunted her at times, and tonight they came floating back.

I kept the locket, Rosie. I kept it. I couldn't get rid of it. I kept it for her. I kept it for her.

Frustrated, Giselle shook her head. She didn't want to think about his affair or how he'd lied to Grandmama. If only she could talk to someone about it. She knew she couldn't talk to her cousins. What if they told their mums and they told Grandmama? No, she couldn't tell anyone in the family. She would have to trust her friends and tell them. She knew that Quinn and Indigo would keep her secret. Besides, her heart would burst if she didn't let it out somehow soon.

Determined, she opened the locket and stared at the laughing baby and at the beautiful blonde woman. She wondered where they were now. Did Nonno's love affair know he had passed away? Was it a love affair? Or was it something else?

Giselle shut the locket, tossed it back into its pouch, and placed it into her schoolbag. Now that it was out of sight, she felt much better. Turning the light off, she turned to one side and tried to go back to sleep, but each time she closed her eyes, images of the long, thin hands danced in her mind. Who knew if she would get any sleep tonight.

It was late when Giselle woke up. The next hour was frantic as she ran around getting herself ready for school. She had struggled to wake up. After the nightmare, she had wrestled to fall asleep. It was probably past three in the morning when she finally dozed off. When her alarm sounded two hours later, she had pressed snooze a few times and didn't crawl out of bed until 6:30. She skipped her morning ride to the lighthouse, did a perfunctory five-minute devotional, had a two-minute shower, wished her mum good luck at her new job, and bolted to the bus stop. Her stomach dropped as she rounded the corner and saw the bus pull away. Giselle sprinted after it with her hands outstretched. "Hey, hey, come back!" She stopped and gulped in some deep breaths.

Her day was not going well. Tears welled in her eyes. What was wrong with her? It wasn't even that time of the month yet. Reluctantly, she decided to wait for the next bus to come. She looked at the time on her phone and realised she would have to wait an hour. That would make her late to her first class, which happened to be art. *Great!* she thought. *As if I need to miss that lesson.*

Feeling frustrated, tired, and alone, Giselle texted her friends and told them she would be late. They responded that they wished they had cars to pick her up, but she told them not to stress, she was fine.

Giselle pulled her earphones out of her bag and plugged them into her phone. She chose a music playlist, crossed her arms, and waited for the bus to arrive.

The sound of a booming horn alarmed her. She jumped from the bench. How had she dozed off?

"Hey, Giselle," a male voice called.

Giselle's eyes widened, and her lips formed an *O*. "Jace?" She gulped. "What are you doing here?"

Jace grinned his lazy, cute smile, "I'm going to work and saw you sleeping at the bus stop." He let out a big, hearty laugh.

She felt her face burn. "Oh," she managed to say.

"Did you miss your bus or something?" he asked.

She nodded. "Yeah, it's not been a good morning."

"Want a ride?" He pointed behind him to where she could sit behind him on his motorbike.

Her stomach dropped as she stood there debating whether or not she should accept his offer.

"You'll be on time," he added.

She looked at her phone again and saw there were still twenty minutes before the bell. School was only fifteen minutes away. She would be on time if she took his offer.

"Okay, yes, please." She quickly threw her phone and headphones into her bag and walked over to him. His black-and-khaki bike looked huge, and suddenly she felt intimidated.

"I don't have a helmet." When he laughed, she bit her lips and frowned.

"Lift up the seat and you'll find one there," he said.

She lifted the seat, and sure enough, there was a helmet just her size. Feeling clumsy, she put on the shiny khaki helmet, clasped it, and sat behind him.

"You need to hold on," he instructed as he brought the engine to life.

Giselle stretched her arms a few times and then pinched the edges of his jacket to hold on. She didn't feel comfortable wrapping her arms around him.

The engine roared to life, and Jace took off. She squealed as she was jerked from the seat and quickly wrapped her arms around his waist.

He turned his head slightly to her and grinned.

She smiled and held on as if her life depended on it. Which . . . it really did.

As Jace rounded a corner, she closed her eyes and held on more tightly. She knew if she let go, she would topple to the ground.

As the bike flew past Uncle Mick's house, Giselle turned and saw the Uber driving out of the driveway. Her eyes rounded. It was her mum!

She turned her face away and hid in his leather jacket.

A few seconds later she turned around again, but the car had left. That was a close call. Her mum would strangle her if she saw her behind a strange guy's motorbike.

"Just to Charlotte Bay High?" he shouted above the wind.

Giselle hoped he could tell she was nodding, then shouted a weak "yes" just in case he couldn't.

Thirteen minutes later, she stood outside the school gate, took the helmet off, placed it back under the seat, and turned to look at him. "Thank you so much, Jace. Truly you saved me!"

He shrugged. "It was nothing. Glad to help."

"Okay, I better go before the bell. See you tomorrow at Kim's."

He nodded and winked. "See you then." With that, he U-turned and zoomed back down the street.

Giselle stood frozen for a few moments *What just happened?* She took a few gulps of air and headed to her locker.

Indigo was the first one to see her. "Gi, you made it on time!"

Behind her Quinn squealed and ran towards her.

Giselle exhaled. "I was freaking out. It has not been a good morning, except . . ." She paused, a smile creeping across her lips.

"Okay, you are totally bright red. What happened?" Indigo leaned in to inspect her face.

Giselle giggled and moved backwards.

Quinn gasped. "It's about that guy, isn't it? I mean, you just giggled like you're in love. Spill it out!"

Giselle opened the locker door and shoved her bag into it. "Okay yes, it's the guy. His name's Jace, by the way. But hold on. I'll get my books and tell you everything. Let's just say, my legs are barely holding me up."

Quinn and Indigo squealed and clapped. "Aw, that is sooo cute!"

After she grabbed her books and shut the locker, Giselle leaned her head against the door. "He gave me a lift and dropped me at the school gate." She sighed.

Indigo's blue eyes seemed to pop out of her head. "What?! How? Oh my goodness, I'm dying here."

Quinn grabbed Giselle's arm and squeezed it. "On his bike? You rode on his motorbike?" She gaped and ran her other hand through her messy, layered short bob.

Giselle opened her mouth to speak, but the annoying school bell interrupted her words.

"I'll tell you as we walk," she said.

They walked to roll class, and Giselle told them everything, from waking up late to Jace dropping her off at school.

"Did you have to wrap your arms around him and declare your undying love?" Quinn and Indigo chuckled and fluttered their eyelashes.

Giselle rolled her eyes and slapped their arms. "Well, duh! If I hadn't, I would have fallen off the bike." She turned around as the teacher asked them to walk in. "And no, I didn't declare my undying love," she said in a rushed whisper, hiding a smile.

It had felt nice to wrap her arms around him. He had made her feel secure and not alone this morning.

By the time recess came, Giselle was still floating on "Cloud Jace." Her friends snapped their fingers in front of her to grab her attention.

"Gi, you are a goner," Indigo snickered as she opened her locker door and took out a packet of chips.

Giselle sighed. She had tried hard to get him out of her mind, but he just popped in anytime he wanted to. Why was she so attracted to him anyway?

"Ohhh, your hot cousin is coming this way," Indigo whispered as she tucked a strand of her long jet-black hair behind her ear.

Giselle turned around and saw Josh coming her way with Relina, Josh's major crush. "Hey," she said with a grin.

"Hey, Gi. Hey, Indi and Quinn." Josh's lazy smile seemed to make her friends tongue-tied.

Giselle said hi to Relina, who then talked with Indi and Quinn for a bit. Josh cleared his throat and whispered into her ear, "I saw you come on a motorbike this morning." He pursed his lips.

Giselle laughed. "It's okay, Josh. My friends know about it."

He relaxed. "Oh, okay. Cool. So, who is he?"

"Just a guy I know." She shifted her weight from one foot to the other.

"I just want to know if he's legit. Do we even know him?" Josh looked around to make sure no one was eavesdropping.

Giselle put both of her hands on his shoulders. "Relax, Joshy. He's harmless and really nice. He was giving me a ride because I missed my bus this morning. He actually saved me!"

Josh removed his sports cap and scratched his light brown hair, so much lighter than the twins' chocolate brown mops. "Okay, you're a good judge of character, but you need to be careful. I have to meet this guy."

Giselle laughed. "Sure, Joshy," she said.

As he walked off, Giselle could not help but feel safe and loved by her family. Her cousin was the kindest guy.

Indigo stared after Josh, and when he was out of earshot, she placed her hands on her chest and said, "He is just too dreamy!" She turned again to take one last look. "How did Relina get so lucky?" She moaned.

Giselle laughed and continued taking out her lunch from her bag. She knew Josh was right. He was worried about her. She hoped he wouldn't tell the twins yet or, even worse, her mum. Giselle took her phone out of her locker and did a quick check of her messages. One had come through from her mum.

GO TO THE OFFICE AND RING ME AS SOON AS YOU GET THIS TEXT.

Giselle gulped. Busted! She was dead.

Chapter 13

After she reread the text to her friends, Giselle dashed to the front office to ring her mum. She asked Mrs. Eaton if she could take the cordless phone outside for privacy. The receptionist hesitated a moment but then consented.

After she punched in the last number, Giselle stood still as the phone rang.

"Hello, this is Lousiana Hayes."

"Mum."

"Oh, Giselle, I have been so worried about you." Her mum sounded stressed.

"What's wrong?" Giselle fumbled with one of the buttons on the blouse of her uniform.

"I was sure I saw you riding on some guy's motorbike this morning." Her mum's voice was strained. "But I could not see your face. I know my own daughter, but oh, I don't know, maybe it was first-day jitters." One word stumbled over the other.

Giselle tapped her foot nervously and wrestled with the idea of admitting it was her on the bike, finally deciding to deny it.

"I'm glad you're okay and it wasn't you on that bike." Her mother exhaled audibly.

Giselle changed the subject. "Ma, how's your first day going?"

"Honey, I am loving this so much. Your uncle Cameron was right about this job. I'm glad he told me about it. Well I'd better get back to work. Love you."

"Love you." Giselle heard the click and held the phone to her ear a little longer.

Regret filled her heart. Why hadn't she just told her mum the truth? She should have just admitted it had been her on the bike. She needed to tell her the truth. She did not want to add another lie to her other one. Lying about her job was bad enough. What must God think of her?

The bell for the end of recess interrupted her cascade of thoughts. Without wasting another second, she rushed into the office, handed the phone back to Mrs. Eaton, thanked her, and hurried to her next class.

On her way past a year 12 class, she saw Emily waving. "I'll text you tonight," Emily mouthed.

Giselle gave her a thumbs-up and headed into her math classroom. It sounded like Emily had found out about the bike and Jace. Giselle shrugged. Oh well, that was her life. Everyone knew everyone's business. It was part of being in the Hayes family. No one kept secrets from each other in her family.

By the time school finished and she was on her way to the bus stop, she was too exhausted to go to Grandmama's house. She would have to wait and go Wednesday afternoon. She yawned and closed her eyes for a few seconds.

A car horn made her head jerk sideways. "Hey, Gi, want a ride?" The sound of Emily's voice made her grin, and she jumped up from her seat.

"Yes, please." She wiped the sweat from her forehead and hurried to get into the car.

The luxury of the cool air con melted her heat away, and instantly she relaxed. "Thank you so much! It's boiling hot." Giselle placed her boho bag onto the floor of the car and leaned her head back against the car seat. "Where's Kiki?" she asked.

"She's working on some assignment with Relina. They've gone to her house." Emily pulled out of the bus stop area and headed towards Charlotte Bay Marina.

"Gi, seriously, we can pick you up in the mornings, you know." Emily turned her music up a little bit.

Giselle shook her head. "You know Mum doesn't allow it. She says we are not a charity case and doesn't want us to be a burden to others."

"But we're family! We're not weirdos or strangers." Emily moved the air con nob a little higher.

"It's not you or anything. It's her weird thinking." Giselle shifted in the front seat to look at Emily. "Well, it's her thing to prove Grandmama wrong."

Emily turned her pretty face towards Giselle. Her blue-grey eyes narrowed, and her messy bun wobbled on top of her head. It looked slightly angry, like Emily in that moment. "Please explain."

Giselle nodded. "Ever since Grandmama told her not to go to Europe all those years ago, Mum has been wanting to show Grandmama that she's an independent and reliable woman. Then she married Dad and did not want a single dollar from Nonno or Grandmama. She said she wanted to do this married life thing on her own." Giselle touched her short, paint-smeared nails and tried to scrape off a little of the paint she had used in art that morning.

"Okay, so how does all that not let us drive you?" Emily asked as she turned right at the traffic light.

"Well, it's because Grandmama used to tell her that Dad was a penniless artist and that she had married wrong. When Daddy died, Mum made a promise to herself that she would never take charity from any of the family. Even when we lived with Nonno and Grandmama, she still paid rent and everything else. Anyways, she says she wants me to grow up independent and not rely on anyone. Oh, and guess what? I'm going to start learning to drive. Mum insists I learn and get my license. I'm kind of excited."

Emily smiled. "Oh, Gi, that'll be awesome. You have to drive. I mean, your mum doesn't, so you will need to."

"Mum knows how to drive, but after Dad died in that car crash, she has been completely traumatised for life at the thought of driving. She says that Ubers are perfect for her," Giselle explained.

"Yeah, and a total waste of money. Not to mention who might be picking you up." Emily snorted. "Now, onto a juicier subject, I heard about you and that guy today!" Emily turned her face towards Giselle and said, "I know everything."

Giselle groaned. "Did Josh tell you?"

"Josh knows?" Emily turned the music down.

"Well, yeah. He saw me this morning getting a ride from 'that guy,' but who told *you*?"

"I have my sources." Emily chuckled, exaggerating her laugh to sound like a mad professor doing an evil experiment.

"Okay, fine. Yes, I was running late this morning, and he saw me at the bus stop and offered to give me a ride. I said yes. It was all innocent." Giselle didn't know why she felt defensive.

"Gi, he likes you. It's not innocent. I mean, you are, but he isn't." Emily beeped at a guy on a bike who crossed in front of her without signalling. "Hey, watch it. I could have flattened you!"

Giselle frowned. "What do you mean 'he isn't'?"

"Only that he definitely likes you and will ask you out, sooner or later. Mark my words." She turned into Uncle Mick's driveway.

Giselle chuckled. "He won't ask me out, trust me. We barely know each other."

Emily parked in front of the house, unbuckled her seat belt, and turned to Giselle. "We need a cousin breakfast so you can fill us in with the rest of the details. When can we meet up?"

Giselle unfastened her seat belt and grabbed her bag. "I start working at Kim's Café this week, so I won't have time. Maybe Saturday night? And we can go bowling."

Emily shook her head. "Ezi hates bowling. She says it ruins her nails, or weapons, as I call them. Those things could gouge an eye out." Emily shivered.

Giselle laughed. Exactly her thoughts. "Okay, so how about we go on a picnic Saturday afternoon or Sunday lunch?"

"Yes, yummy. That works. I'll organise it and text everyone," Emily said. "I can't wait."

"We can video call Soph," Giselle added.

The girls said goodbye, and Giselle stood on the steps and watched Emily drive away.

The picnic sounded awesome.

She opened the sophisticated French door and went straight upstairs to change and have something to eat. The silence of the house felt a little spooky when she came downstairs. She turned the light switch on and let the chandelier come to life and illuminate the hallway. She turned the stereo on and played some music. The beautiful melody filled the empty space and chased the loneliness away. Suddenly she did not feel so alone.

Dear Diary,

I totally forgot to tell Quinn and Indi about the locket and my crazy nightmare. Grr, it's because my head was filled with Jace. Jace, Jace, Jace. All day that's all I've thinking about. It's so frustrating to like someone that I barely know, but the fact that he seems to like me, too, is the best! I was not looking to like a guy or anything, so it's really not my fault. It just happened naturally. I actually have knots in my stomach. Tomorrow I get to see him during my shift. I start work at four in the afternoon and finish at seven. Which works out PERFECT because Mum won't be home till around eight thirty. Plenty of time to pretend I have been home all afternoon. I feel totally guilty, but I have to get over it. Europe and my dad await.

Giselle paused her writing when she heard the door downstairs open. She looked at her alarm clock, which read 8:35 p.m. It must be her mum back from work. She knew it wasn't her uncle, for he was away for a few more days. Feeling happy, Giselle closed her half-finished diary entry and rushed to meet her mum. She could hardly wait to hear all about her new job. She hoped that this time her mum would settle down and stick to it. That way she could save up and buy the little beach house they both wanted. As she rushed out her door, she remembered she'd left the locket on her bed. She rushed back, put it back into its pouch, and hid the pouch in her bag. Tomorrow she would be sure to tell her friends all about it.

Chapter 14

"**Y**ou guys, I have to tell you something very . . ." Giselle's voice trailed off as she waited for some other students to walk past her. "It's an enormous secret. It's killing me, and I need to tell someone."

It was Tuesday lunchtime, and Giselle and her friends sat at their usual place under the big shade tree near the art room. It was secluded and kept them hidden from the burning summer sun.

Quinn shifted her petite figure and leaned forward. Her dark eyes widened. "Gi, you know we would never tell"

Indigo nodded and pretended to zip her lips and throw away the key. "We are tombs," she said as she crossed her impossibly long legs.

Giselle opened her bag and withdrew the little pouch. She untied the drawstrings and took out the locket. Gasps of admiration escaped her friends' lips.

"It's super gorgeous." Indi ran her index finger over the dragonfly. "Where did you get it?"

Quinn took it from Indigo and whistled. She sounded exactly like one of her three little brothers when she whistled like that. Giselle looked at Indigo, and they both laughed.

"Okay, so the secret," Giselle lowered her voice. "The morning before my Nonno died, he told me I had to read a book of his. Except he didn't recognise me and kept calling me the nickname he had for Grandmama." Giselle took a deep breath. "He then kept screaming and shouting that he had lied to me. Well, to Rosie, my grandma. He was ballistic and kept shouting that I had to forgive him. So, I did." Giselle wiped the tears from her cheeks.

Indigo reached over and grabbed her hand. "I'm so sorry, Gi."

Giselle tried to smile. "Anyways, I found the book just recently, in my Nonno's garden shed, and this locket was hidden in it."

Quinn lifted the top of the locket and showed Indigo. They stared at Giselle with blank expressions.

"It looks like Nonno had an affair with that blonde woman. I don't think Grandmama ever found out." Giselle wiped her eyes and thanked Quinn, who'd handed her a tissue. Quinn always kept tissues, chocolates, and lollies for her little brothers. "I can't tell my family about the affair. They would never believe me."

"You won't even tell Sophie?" Quinn frowned. "I mean, you two are like sisters. She would definitely understand."

Giselle shook her head vigorously. Her side plait bounced from side to side. "No. I'm too scared."

Her friends nodded.

"Have you seen the woman before?" Indigo asked.

Giselle nodded. "She looks familiar. Nonno used to take me to the park, and I'm sure I saw her with him. I can't remember all the details. I've also decided to find her."

Indigo nodded. "Where will you begin to look for her?"

"I might try Google and see if I can find information on her. Look at this." Giselle pointed to the other black-and-white photo. "It looks like she had a baby."

"Do you think your Nonno might have more hidden photos of that woman?" Indi asked as she packed her lunchbox into her bag.

Giselle shrugged. "I have no idea. But I'm going to Grandmama's this week to find some photo inspiration for my art assignment. I'll see if I can find more photos. I mean, she could have been a family friend, I guess."

The bell rang too soon, and the girls had to hurry to their next classes. Giselle felt emotionally exhausted and was even not looking forward to her first shift at Kim's Deli Café. But the sudden thought of seeing Jace again made her stomach flip-flop. It might be a good shift after all.

Dear Diary,

I am dead tired! But my heart is happy. I got Jace's number, and he got mine. My goodness, I have to tell you EVERYTHING that happened at Kim's today.

So, I finished school and headed to Kim's Café. Kiki and Emily couldn't drop me off because they had after-school things today. Josh took me instead. He offered to drop me off so I wouldn't be late to my first day at work. I made him promise not to tell anyone. Of course, he's a guy and shrugged off my instructions. But I know he won't spill. As soon as I walked in, I went to change into my uniform. I also put the little daisy brooch on my collar. This brooch kind of makes me feel like my dad is close to me.

I made sure I arrived ten minutes before my shift. I wanted time to calm down before I started work. My nerves were everywhere.

Jace was on an afternoon break, so I didn't see him when I first got there. I was bummed—Kim wasn't there either, but the rock chick, the one from my interview, was there to show me the ropes. Talia (that's her name) was nice, a bit edgy, and all business but okay. She introduced me to the other workers. I met Halee, who is super pretty with her almond-shaped eyes and straight black hair. She is sooo nice! Halfway through the introduction, Jace walked in. Talia then introduced me to Jace. He winked at me when no one was looking. I met Devon, the head chef. He's got red hair and tattoos down his arm and neck. I can just see Grandmama's face if she saw him, LOL! But he's super, super nice. I think there's a thing between Talia and him. The way they look at each other— whoa, fire.

When my shift started, Halee took me with her to take orders. There's a system to taking orders, and I felt nervous. But by the last thirty minutes of my shift, I actually got to do a full order all by myself. Halee was serving other customers, and I had to go on my own. Aah, I almost died! But I survived. I only got two orders wrong and broke one plate. Halee said it was not bad for a first shift. Phew.

Okay, so the juicy part . . . When my shift was over, I headed to the break room to change out of my apron and gather my things. Jace turned up as I grabbed my schoolbag. He grinned. I melted. I have to write it out exactly as it happened. It was amazing!

"Hey, Giselle," he said, leaning against the wall, his arms crossed. "How'd your shift go?"

I shrugged and spread my hands. "I'm not sure what Talia would think, but I did okay. Except I mixed up two orders and broke a plate." I grimaced.

He laughed. "That's pretty good. On my first shift, I dropped a whole tray of dirty dishes and splashed water on several customers. I thought I'd get fired."

I gasped. "Yikes, that sounds awful! Lucky Kim kept you."

He nodded and shifted his weight to the other leg. "Kim's really cool. She gave me another chance and told me it was all part of learning. So, when's your next shift?"

"Thursday after school," I said. "You?"

He pursed his lips. "I work every day."

I wanted to ask if he went to school or the university, but I didn't have the guts. I still don't know him really well.

"Hey, I was wondering if you could give me your number?" He uncrossed his arm and ran his hand through his hair.

I stared at him. Should I? I thought to myself.

"Um, just so . . . I mean, in case you need to contact me for something. Or you're late to your shift. I can help out," he said in a rush.

"Okay, sure?" I rolled my eyes. Seriously, why did I answer like a question? How dumb.

We exchanged numbers, and as I reached to get my phone back, our fingers touched. I moved my hand back as if I had touched fire. But he held on to the phone and stared at my face. His face was close enough for me to see how his eyes glowed. I glanced at my feet and tucked a flyaway strand of hair behind my ear.

107

"Thank you," he said softly and handed the phone back.

I knew my face must have been the colour of the beetroot sandwich I had served that day.

We chatted some more, but when I noticed the time, I told him I had to go home.

We said bye, and I floated out the door. I don't even remember walking home. LOL.

Mum hasn't come home yet. She texted that she was running late, which gave me time to shower and get the smell of food out of my clothes. Lying is so exhausting and frustrating. Anyways, I'm off to unwrap my towelled head and braid my hair.

—G

Giselle bit the edge of her pen and smiled as she relived the look Jace gave her. She turned her attention back to her journal and drew a love heart and a few clouds below her entry. She giggled and shut the book.

After brushing her hair, she saw a missed call from Sophie and a text from Rachel, her mentor from church.

She texted Rachel back and thanked her for asking about the job. Then she called Sophie.

"Gi! I miss you!" the voice on the other end exclaimed.

Giselle smiled. "Soph, miss you more. I can't wait till you come home."

"Me too! Oh, and just so you know, for Christmas I'm going to get you a brand-new phone with FaceTime and everything. Your phone is a dinosaur, and I can't even see you." Sophie moaned on the other end.

Giselle could just see her bow-shaped lips pouting and her pretty face wrinkled in mock horror and disgust.

Giselle laughed. "Don't be so dramatic, Soph. My phone is fine. Mum gave it to me, remember? I can't throw it out."

"She gave it to you because she got a new one. It's old. When I give you the new one, you need to get Instagram so we can video chat."

Giselle grimaced. "Ugh, no way. I hate social media. Do you know the dramas that happen on that thing? No thanks!"

She heard Sophie exhale. "Fine! But a new phone will come for Christmas."

Giselle didn't feel like arguing. She knew, when Sophie made up her mind, it was impossible to change it.

"So, tell me everything. How was your first day at Kim's?" Sophie squealed into the phone.

"You'd better sit, Soph."

Sophie squealed again, and Giselle rolled her eyes. Her cousin was a true romantic.

For the next hour the girls chatted about school, work, and guys.

"Guess what, Gi," Sophie said. "You know how there's a public holiday coming up?"

"Yes."

"Dad said I can go home for it." Sophie shrieked.

Giselle let out a holler. "That's the best news ever, Soph!"

They were in the middle of their conversation when Giselle heard the front door open and a car drive off. Her mum was home.

"Okay, Soph. Gotta run. Mum's home."

"Say hi to Aunty Lusi for me," Sophie instructed.

"Will do."

They both hung up, and Giselle headed downstairs to have a chat with her mum. It was becoming their tradition to sit outside on the veranda, have tea, and talk at the end of the day. Giselle was beginning to like this nightly routine.

"Hey, Ma," she called as she headed downstairs.

Her mum's heels were on the lustrous marble floor in one corner along with her scarf, jacket, and handbag.

"Hi, honey. The tea is almost ready." Her mum's voice floated from the kitchen.

Giselle went into the kitchen and hugged her hello.

"Before I ask you about school, I wanted to ask if you're free this Thursday after school?" Her mum's bare feet made tiny sounds as she scurried around the kitchen getting things ready.

Giselle gaped. Thursday? That was her second shift at Kim's.

"Um, not really," she managed to say.

"It's just that I'm going to finish work early that day and wanted to see if we could go shopping. I need new clothes, and you do too." The kettle whistled.

"Yeah, I'm kind of busy. Maybe Sunday morning after breakfast?" Giselle shifted from one foot to the other.

Her mum nodded. "Sure. That'd be perfect."

Giselle exhaled and followed her mum outside. For now she would just enjoy the tea, her mum, and the lovely view of the lit-up marina.

Chapter 15

Wednesday came and went too fast for Giselle, and since she was home from school early, she decided to go for a ride and hang out at the lighthouse. The day was a little overcast, and for a second, Giselle stood at the garage door before venturing out. Was a storm brewing? She googled the weather and saw there was a possibility of rain, but no storm was in the forecast. Filled with relief, she took her art book and sketching pens and biked towards the lighthouse. The cool breeze whirled through her hair, and she smiled at the beauty of the ocean. She should paint it and hang the picture in her room. Then she grimaced: her mum did not let her hang anything on the walls. She said she did not want to ruin Uncle Mick's immaculate mansion. That was another reason Giselle wished they were living in their own house. She would hang paintings everywhere.

An hour later Giselle stared at her self-portrait sketch. "Ugh," she groaned. She was not impressed. At this rate, she was going to get a big fat zero and fail this assignment. Maybe she wasn't meant to be an artist after all. She sighed. Her dad was an artist. Maybe she was just trying to be him and it wasn't going to happen.

The ding of her phone announced a text message. It was from Emily.

HEY GIRLS, SAVE THE DATE FOR THIS SUNDAY 3:00 P.M. WE'RE MAJORLY OVERDUE FOR A CUZ GET TOGETHER. GI HAS SOME GUY GOSSIP TO TELL US—LET'S JUST SAY IT INVOLVES THE CUTE WAITER AND A MOTORBIKE, LOL.

Giselle covered her mouth. Only Em. Trust her to announce her business to the world. At least it was just to the cousins. Emily's text finished with a list of foods they could bring to share.

PS: DON'T BE MEASLY. BRING PLENTY OF FOOD.

Giselle locked her phone as a few drops of rain began to pelt her. She scurried to her bike and rode home as fast as her legs could take her. When a little roll of thunder echoed in the distance, her heart thudded. *No, no, please no storm.* She rode faster. She felt so silly for trusting the weather forecast; Nonno always said God made the decision, not the meteorologist.

By the time she arrived home, she felt like a drowned cat. She wiped her bike dry, tucked it away, and carefully walked upstairs to shower and change.

A rumble echoed far away, but not loud enough to scare her. She just hoped it stayed that way.

After a quick dinner, she headed to her room to do her homework. A wave of loneliness hit her as she sat on the desk chair listening to the rain hit her window. She often wished she had a brother or sister to make her feel more secure, less lonely even.

She shook her head to clear out her thoughts and continued to do her math homework.

Her thoughts drifted again—to her art assignment, to Jace, to Nonno, and to the locket. She could not concentrate. Frustrated, she stood up and went to get the locket. She opened it gently and stared at the photos. Giselle grabbed her art book and began to sketch the woman. She drew each feature in detail, all the while racking her brain as to where she had seen her before. A sudden memory of a park flashed in her mind, and she froze. She remembered little bits and pieces. She was sitting on a swing, and her Nonno was swinging her high. She kept giggling and asking him to go higher and higher. She tried to remember more, but she couldn't. The memory reminded her of her recurring nightmare. Sometimes she saw her dad, and other times she saw Nonno. Then the blonde woman with the strange hands appeared. She was sure the woman in her nightmare was the woman in the locket. Years ago, Nonno used to take her bike riding or to the lake Sunday afternoons, and he always met up with people. Had she seen her at the park or the lake? Was she from church? And how old was she now? Had Nonno had the affair years ago, and had he had the affair for years? Her mind filled with unanswered questions—she had to find out something. She closed the locket again and wrote the initials engraved on the front—O. A. B.—under the sketch. Could that be the woman's name? Giselle wrote down every female church member whose name started with the letter *O*.

Olga, Ophelia, Opal, Olive, Odelia, and Orialia. There weren't that many, but at least her list of names was a start to her investigation. She would keep an eye on them this weekend. Giselle checked her list again and crossed out Opal; she was only a baby. Now she had only five names to work with.

She closed her art book, put the locket back into the pouch, and the pouch into her schoolbag.

She looked at her clock; it read 8:00 p.m. Good, her mum would be home any minute. Giselle went downstairs and got the tea and some crackers and cheese ready for their nightly chat. She loved these moments, but she wished her mum would talk more about Dad.

The next afternoon, Giselle waved goodbye to Kiki, who'd given her a ride, and disappeared inside Kim's for her shift. Her mum had texted her letting her know she would be home by five o'clock this afternoon and would wait for her to arrive so they could have dinner together. Dreading every word, Giselle texted back that she had an assignment to finish and was going with a friend to the local library. She said she would be home by seven thirty.

The bell above her head jingled as she entered the café. It sounded like it was calling out, "Liar, liar!" Giselle shuddered. She did not have time for this guilt right now. She waved to Halee, who was behind the counter serving a customer, and called hello to Devon, the chef, who stuck his head out the kitchen window and called hello to her.

She liked him. Giselle pushed open the swinging door of the break room and bumped straight into Jace.

"Hi!" She blushed at the sound of her excited voice. *Settle down,* she told herself. *Don't sound desperate.*

Jace grinned lazily as he untied the back of his apron. "Hey, Giselle, good to see you." His green eyes sparkled.

Giselle watched him hang the apron onto the rack with his name above it. "You're leaving?" She tried to sound natural.

"Yeah, my shift's over."

"Oh." She hoped he couldn't hear the bitter disappointment in her voice. The smile drained from her face.

He flashed a grin. "I actually finished an hour ago, but I wanted to see you."

"You did?"

He nodded. "I'm glad I stuck around till you got here," he said softly.

Giselle gulped. "Me too," she whispered.

"By the way, you look beautiful," Jace said. "I love your hair out like that."

She looked at her shoes self-consciously and ran a hand through her wavy tresses. Her scrunchie had come undone, and she hadn't had time to do her hair up again.

"Thanks." She smiled at him.

"By the way, I was wondering if you'd like to hang out this weekend?" Jace fixed his eyes on her.

Giselle froze. What could she say? She would love to go on a date with him, but she would never be allowed. Her mother was strict when it came to boys and dating.

"Oh, I would love to, but . . ." She paused. "I have church this weekend, and I'm going shopping with my mum, and then I have a picnic with my cousins." She wondered if she could cancel the picnic. "Unless you want to hang out at church with me and then come have lunch at my grandmother's house." She tilted her head to the side, hopeful he would say yes.

Jace stepped back. "Um, I don't really do church, at all. I don't think I could hang out there, you know."

She nodded. "Of course, yeah, that's totally fine." She wished she would have never mentioned church.

"How about next weekend?" he asked.

She grinned. "It's a date!" She gasped. "I mean, it's not a date, it's a hangout date. I mean . . ."

Jace threw his head back and laughed. "It's a date!" he said and winked at her.

Giselle laughed and watched as he walked out.

Her heart boomed in her chest, and she leaned her head against the wall to catch her breath. She couldn't wait to tell her friends and cousins the latest.

By the time Giselle crawled into her soft bed that night, she was dying. Having full-time school and a part-time job was not easy. How was she going to survive the year? How was she ever going to get her assignments done on time? Maybe her mum had been right after all; maybe she should just concentrate on her studies. Giselle rubbed some lavender oil on her temples and behind her ears, turned off her lamp, and went to sleep.

"Higher, Daddy, higher!" Giselle shouted above the roaring wind.

Her dad fixed his glasses and shouted, "Yes!" She felt like she was flying high up with the birds.

Suddenly a clap of thunder shook her, and she yelled for her dad to bring the swing to a stop. Her dad stopped the swing, and as he turned around, she saw the face of her Nonno.

"Nonno!" she gasped.

She closed her eyes for a brief second and looked at him again, but this time it was her dad's face again. Filled with confusion, Giselle tried to break free of her swing seat, but she was trapped. She wiggled and squirmed. "Get me out! Get me out!" she yelled.

All of a sudden, long strange hands reached for her, grabbing her around the waist. "I've got you. I'll take you out." The stranger's voice and hands filled Giselle with panic, and she kicked her legs like a wild horse.

"Don't touch me!" she screamed.

The stranger leaned forward and moved close to Giselle's face. "It's okay," she said.

Giselle inhaled.

The blonde hair. The face. The smile. It was *her*. The woman in the locket.

Giselle woke up with a start and sat up in bed. Her hands trembled as she fumbled with the light switch on her lamp.

The soft glow of the light spilled into her room, and she breathed deeply. She had seen her, and she had talked to her, the woman in the locket. She had seen Nonno, too, and her dad.

Giselle buried her face in her hands and cried. She was over this nightmare. She had to tell her cousins on Sunday. She would leave out her suspicions about the affair but would tell them about her nightmare.

Chapter 16

Dear Diary,

I saw her! I saw Nonno's love affair. I went to church and I kept my eyes peeled for the list of women with the letter O who were there. There was one in particular who caught my attention: Ophelia. She had blonde hair with white streaks through it. She didn't really look like the woman in the locket photo, but that photo was ages ago, so she wouldn't look like that now. She was sitting with a man with a fully grey beard and another grown man, perhaps their son. My eyes bulged, and my stomach dropped. Could Ophelia be the one Nonno had an affair with? At the end of the church service, I went past her and said hi. She smiled politely but continued talking to her son. I was intrigued, so I walked over to talk to Grandma so I could keep an eye on her. I asked Grandmama if she knew much about Ophelia, but she said no. She said Ophelia had never really liked her. "She loved your Nonno, though," she said. I gulped. The more I saw her, the more I suspected her. I need to tell Indi and Quinn.

Uh, I also went shopping with Mum. Got some cute clothes. While we were out, I got a text from Jace saying hi (I nearly passed out!), and now I'm getting ready to go to the park for our cuz picnic. I can't wait. It's been way too long since we've been together. I haven't seen Ezi or Silver for ages. Okay, so only a few weeks, but it feels way too long. And I was supposed to go to Grandma's house to see the albums, but I didn't have time on Friday. I guess I'll have to go Monday after school.

Oh, guess what? Mum talked about getting a loan so she could buy a house. I mean our own house. We've never had one. When we came back from England, we lived with Nonno and Grandmama and then moved to live with Uncle Mick. I can't imagine having my own room. I have so many plans already. I want to paint the walls of my room. I can so see the decor already. White and yellow and of course splashes of green, plus I want to hang peacock feathers on one side and in the other corner a hammock hanging from the ceiling, pretty with lace and prints and a big cushion on my bed. It would be even better if I had a loft room. The possibilities are endless. Mum told me not to mention it to anyone yet. She wants to investigate first. She'll tell Uncle Mick 'cause he's going to with her to get the loan, but no one else must know. Bummer, I wish I could tell my cousins, but I can't yet.

Anyways, I'd better go get the sushi ready. Mum bought a huge platter of assorted sushi rolls so I can share. We don't want Emily going hungry. LOL. Okay, I'd better get going. The twins are picking me up soon. I can't wait!

—G

Giselle drew a little picnic basket and a blanket in the corner of the page, closed the book, hid it under her

120

pillow, and hurried downstairs. Just as she descended the stairs, she heard the car horn.

"Ah, they're here." She bolted to the kitchen and grabbed the covered platter.

"Honey, take it easy. Don't drop that platter," her mum said as she followed her out the door.

"I won't, Ma. Bye." She gave her mum a quick peck on the cheek and walked carefully down the steps. She paused halfway and said, "By the way, Ma, don't forget that I'm going to hang out with the twins after the picnic. I'll be home around nine."

"Sure, honey, enjoy." Her mum blew her a kiss as she got into the car.

Giselle bit her bottom lip. How she hated to lie. There was no way she could tell her mum she was working tonight.

She looked out the window and waved goodbye.

Giselle watched each of her cousins' faces as they sat spellbound with the details she told them about Jace. Emily's sushi was halfway to her mouth, but she was not eating.

"But he seems nice, and we are hanging out next Sunday."

Giselle's squeal broke the spell of her cousins, and they squealed along with her.

"Oh, Gi, just be careful. He isn't Christian or anything." Silver hoisted her long ginger hair into a bun and proceeded to take a long drink of her juice.

Kiki nodded in agreement. "Okay, so don't get mad at me or anything, but I didn't like how opposed to going to church he was when you asked him."

"He wasn't opposed as such," Ezi piped up. "He was reluctant but not opposed." She tapped her newly painted long black nails on the edge of her drink bottle. Her impossible curls sat on top of her head, commanding attention.

Giselle supressed a smile. Ezi's curls were just as dramatic and attention seeking as Ezi was.

"Shockingly, I'm with Ezi," Emily said between mouthfuls of chips and spicy capsicum dip. "I think church is something he isn't used to, and he's afraid to go. But that could change."

Kiki gasped. "Traitor," she muttered.

Everyone laughed and the mood lifted.

The need to change the subject was evident. Giselle said, "Also, I need to tell you something else."

Sophie, who was joining them via video, tapped her screen. "Turn me a little to the left so I can see you all better," she said.

Emily moved the phone a little to the left and added another cushion behind it. "Is that better?" she asked.

Sophie gave her a thumbs-up.

"Go on, Gi," Ezi said.

"For the last few weeks," Giselle began, "I've been having a really strange dream. Actually, it's more like a nightmare, and it wakes me up every time. It's so creepy." She looked down at her hands and tried to remove the smudge of lead that decorated the side of her right one.

"I don't know what it is or why I'm dreaming it, but it's driving me nuts."

"What's the dream about?" Sophie asked as she leaned close to the screen, her blue eyes wide with anticipation.

"I'm sitting on a swing, and there's laughter all around me. It looks like I'm at a park somewhere, and I can see my dad." Giselle smiled as her mind travelled to her father. "I keep telling him to push me higher. He does, and I feel like I'm flying. Then it starts to rain, and a storm starts brewing. I get so scared and scream and yell for him to take me out of the swing. But I can't move. I feel trapped, and as I struggle on the swing, I see female hands reach out and grab me around the waist. I scream more because I don't recognise the hands. Sometimes I even see Nonno there instead of my dad. It's really creepy and weird." Giselle shivered.

Her cousins were silent until Esmeralda broke the silence. "Okay, I'm not Joseph or anything. I can't interpret dreams . . ." The cousins snickered Esmeralda glared at them and continued. "But to me it sounds like it's coming from your subconscious. Something has definitely triggered this dream."

"Triggered, as in photos or books or something like that?" Silver asked, her face creased with concern.

Esmeralda nodded. "Yes, it's like something woke up those nightmares. And I think the woman you see is someone who has caused pain or damaged someone you love." Ezi crossed her legs on the picnic blanket and smiled in satisfaction at her diagnosis of Giselle's problem.

"Since when did you get so wise, Ezi?" Sophie asked, incredulous.

"You definitely sound legit," Emily agreed. She, too, seemed impressed.

Ezi laughed. "Well, I'm taking psychology at the moment as one of my subjects. And it's actually really cool. I love it."

While her cousins praised her and asked questions about her subject, Giselle sat quietly. She knew what had triggered the nightmares. It was the locket. As for the woman in her dream? Yes, she had hurt someone all right. Her whole family, especially her grandmother. If only she could confront Ophelia and slap her face. She gasped inside. Where had that come from? She did not want to confront or hit anyone.

The conversation continued about the nightmare for a little longer until Kiki suggested she go see the school counsellor to get some tips on how to stop the nightmares. Giselle agreed it could help but said she was not very comfortable talking about it to her quite yet.

"Oh, by the way, changing the subject," Esmeralda said, flicking a curl from her face that had escaped from her bun. "Gi, are you still planning to go to Europe at the end of year twelve?"

"Yes and yes." Giselle clapped her hands. "I'm going to save as much as I can. There's so much to do and buy."

"I'm going with her," Sophie added as she munched on her favourite snack of Tim Tams.

"Have you gotten your passport?" the twins asked in unison. "Jinx!" They poked each other on the arm and burst out laughing.

"Yeah, Gi, you need to get your passport soon," Silver said.

"But I won't need it till next year," Giselle said before popping a handful of peanuts in her mouth.

"Do you know how long getting a passport could take?" Esmeralda leaned forward. "Mum had so many issues when she had to get one for me. There were delays. Trust me, it was nightmarish."

"How long did it take?" Giselle wondered how a piece of paper could be *nightmarish*, as Ezi put it.

"It took six months! So, my advice is for you to get your old passport ASAP. You would have one from England when you came with your mum, and you just need to renew it."

"Don't I need my mum's signature or something?" Giselle cocked her head and frowned.

Ezi shrugged. "I don't know. Just find your old one and start there."

The girls popped up with different passport scenarios while Giselle sat deep in thought. She was sure her mum had it in the safety box in the study downstairs. Giselle had seen her put important papers there.

She made a mental note to check the safety box one night soon.

Dear Diary,

I got home late from work. I had to stay late and finish mopping the floors. Kim said the place has to be impeccable for the morning, Jace actually had a day off on Sunday, so I didn't see him, but he did text me and wished me a good night. Aw, he is so sweet. Anyways, hanging out with the cousins was exactly what I needed. They cheered me up, and for those hours I forgot about lying to Mum, Nonno's affair, the locket, the assignment, and Jace. Well, okay, maybe not Jace. But everything else disappeared in the background and it felt good. I can't wait for our next outing. Ezi's going to organise the next one.

I'm planning on going to Grandmama's house tomorrow and check some photos for my assignment. I'll call her and let her know. I'm sure she'll be cool with it. Oh, and I got a text from Uncle Mick today. He's still in London, and he sent me a photo of the red double-decker buses. I am so jealous. I can't wait to go see them myself. If my dad was still alive, he would do all the tours with me. He would guide me and take me to all the artsy places. He would have made the best tour guide ever.

Giselle paused her writing as her father's face crossed her mind. She pressed her lips together. Life was unfair. She went back to her journal and continued to write.

When I came home, Mum was already in bed, but she left me a note with a love heart and good-night hugs and kisses on it. She also packed my lunch for school tomorrow. She is the sweetest mum in the world. I love her so much, and I'm super happy to see her so thrilled at her new job. I have a great feeling about this job. I think she's finally going to settle down.

All right. I've yawned ten times already. I need to go to sleep. It's way past eleven o'clock.

—G

Giselle drew a little pillow along with "*zzz*" at the end of her entry and closed her book. She reached for her phone and looked at Uncle Mick's photo again.

"Soon, I'll be there," she said. She turned off her light and went to sleep.

Chapter 17

"**A**re you *sure* she is the love affair?" Indigo asked.

It was lunchtime, and Giselle and her friends sat in their usual area under the tree, their lunch boxes sprawled in the middle of their circle as they nibbled from each other's food. Giselle had just filled the girls in about Ophelia, the woman who fit the description of the blonde woman in the locket photo.

Giselle flicked a fly that flew by and replied, "I think so. But I need to find out more info before I actually confront her. I mean, she matches all the things I know so far."

"But you said she looks older? The woman in the photo is young." Quinn took a bite of her Nutella sandwich and cleaned the corner of her mouth.

Indi slapped her arm. "Don't be silly, Quinn!" she said. "That photo is at least ten years old. Gi was like a little girl."

Quinn covered her food-filled mouth and laughed. "Oh," was all she could say between her uncontrollable giggles.

The girls laughed until they turned red. Giselle rolled her eyes. Considering Quinn had three little brothers who kept her on her toes, she could be really daft at times.

"Okay, so as I was about to say," Giselle began, "she fits all the details. She is blonde, now with white through her hair. Giselle tapped the locket photo with her index finger. "And her son could be this baby. Oh, but that isn't everything." Giselle paused and saw her friends' wide eyes staring at her. They leaned forward.

"I asked Grandma about Ophelia, and she told me Ophelia has not liked Grandmama very much, but hear this, she did love Nonno." With those words, Giselle shut the locket with a clunk.

"Oh, wow, that is huge!" Indigo tied her blue-black hair up into a ponytail. "To me it is obvious."

"Dang." Quinn covered the lid of her empty lunch box and placed it back into her bag.

Giselle nodded. "I know. Now I have to think on how I will talk to her and get her to confess. I need ideas."

For the next few minutes, the girls discussed scenarios about how Giselle could casually talk to Ophelia to get information from her. Some of their suggestions made her cringe, others made her laugh hysterically, and others downright terrified her.

The sound of the bell ended their how-to-confront-Ophelia scenarios, and they headed to class.

Her mind filled with questions and doubts. What if she was wrong about Nonno having an affair with Ophelia?

After being nice and cool in air con, Giselle felt like she was suffocating as she waited for the bus to arrive. She was on her way to Grandmother's house to check out some albums and finally get inspired for her art assignment. She had called her after school and given her the news. Grandmama had invited her to stay for dinner, but Giselle had declined. She wanted to get home early enough to work on her assignment and spend time later that night with her mum outside on the veranda.

Giselle checked the time on her phone again and groaned: another twenty minutes before her bus arrived. She took out a piece of paper from her bag and shielded her face from the burning rays of the sun.

The ding of her phone indicated she had a text. Her heart lurched when she saw the name. "Jace." She opened the message and read it.

Hey, Giselle, I just finished my shift. Was wondering if you want to hang out this arvo?

Giselle drew in her breath. Yes, of course she wanted to hang out, but instead, she texted back, Hey! Sorry, I can't. I'm off to my grandma's house to do an assignment. She put a sad emoji face at the end.

Need a ride?

Giselle hesitated. She couldn't ask him to drop her off. Crest Pointe was thirty minutes from Charlotte Bay.

Um, no, I'm good. Thanks.

We can stop to eat somewhere, and then I can drop you off—we can still hang out. Sunday is way too far away.

Giselle bit her bottom lip and tossed the idea back and forth. It would be nice to see him and hang out. It would mean she could get out of the boiling sun and even get to Grandmama's sooner than expected. Squinting, she closed one eye and texted back, Okay. Sounds awesome!

The message disappeared, and she cringed. Too late to change her mind now.

It wasn't long before Jace was at the bus stop near the school where she'd told him she would be. Her heart skipped a beat when she saw the motorbike turn the corner.

Jace took off his helmet and grinned. His shaggy hair was messier than usual but still looked nice. Giselle's nerves vanished at seeing his face, and soon they were off to grab some Mexican food.

Giselle told him to head to Crest Pointe where they had the best Mexican restaurant for miles.

He agreed, and soon she wrapped her arms around his waist and held on tight as they zoomed away.

Giselle hoped no one would recognise her. What would Grandmama and her mum think?

Silver's words came to haunt her: *Oh, Gi, just be careful. He isn't Christian or anything.* Her pretty, freckle-covered face had been genuinely concerned.

Giselle shook her head; she didn't want to think about whether Jace was a Christian or not right now. She simply wanted to enjoy the moment with him.

An hour and a half later, she instructed Jace where to drop her off. "Just here is fine." She pointed to the bus stop island just before turning onto Grandmama's Street.

"You sure?" he asked for the tenth time.

"Totally fine. Grandma would have a fit if I hop off a motorbike in front of her house." Giselle did not want to see that reaction.

Jace brought the bike to a halt and waited for Giselle to get off. He took off his helmet and smiled. "Thanks for hanging out with me today. It was nice."

"Yeah, thanks for asking me." Giselle smiled back. "So, Sunday is off?"

He laughed. "No way. Today was just a bonus date." He grinned, and she laughed.

After waving goodbye, she watched him drive off before she headed to her grandmother's house.

"Darling, you're earlier than I expected you. Come in. Come in." Grandmama encircled her with a big hug and ushered her inside.

"A friend dropped me off," Giselle said.

"How lovely." Grandmama closed the door and walked towards the family room where she kept the albums. "Do you need something to eat or drink?" she asked.

"No, I'm good. My friend and I stopped at the Mexican restaurant." Giselle laid her bag on one of the sofas.

She saw her grandma grimace. "Why didn't you take your friend to Valentina's Tearoom? Such good food and so refined." Grandmama opened the cabinet with the albums.

"Ah he, um, *she* would not have liked the tearoom." Giselle hoped Grandmama hadn't noticed her slipup.

"Oh, is it the girl with the blue-black hair and piercing blue eyes? Yes, you are right. Valentina's Tearoom is *definitely* not for her."

Giselle tried not to laugh at Grandmama's description of Indi.

"You okay if I start the assignment right away?" Giselle didn't want to answer any more questions about her friends, especially since Jace was the one who had dropped her off.

"Of course, darling. I'll get out of your way. Take all the time you need." Grandmama turned and disappeared down the hallway.

Giselle looked through the albums with her mum's name and took the three Grandmama had set aside for her.

For the next hour, Giselle looked through the photos and briefly sketched anything that brought inspiration. She paused at a few and laughed at a group of photos of her mum and Uncle Mick as kids. They were dressed as chickens for probably some church or school event. Uncle Mick did not look impressed. His arms were folded across his chest and his lips pouted. His head was slightly turned, as if he was annoyed by all the silliness. Her mum, on the other hand, had turned her back towards the camera. She'd pushed the chicken tail all the way out. She looked like she was dancing. A huge grin played on her face. Giselle laughed—that was her mum all right, always a bit childish. She drew a brief sketch of that one and added some notes in the corner.

She came across another photo, and her heart stirred. It had been taken at her mum and dad's wedding. Her mum wore a white boho lace dress. A gift from Nonno, she remembered her mum telling her. Her long blonde hair was adorned by a lovely daisy wreath. She looked gorgeous. Her dad also wore all white: white pants and a white short-sleeved formal shirt. A yellow daisy was pinned to his shirt pocket. They were holding a marriage certificate outside the courthouse. Her mum had told her they had a whirlwind romance and had decided to elope and have a civil wedding. Her mum did not want anything fancy or a big fuss to be made. Of course, Grandmama had almost collapsed in shock and fumed that her youngest daughter would not walk down the church aisle and wear a puffy princess dress. Giselle reached for her pencil and sketched the scene. She paused often and stared at her dad's face. How she wished he was alive. Would they be close? Surely they would.

She turned the page and continued looking at more wedding photos.

"Oh," she said, taking in a deep breath.

In another photo, Nonno was laughing at something Mum was saying. Uncle Mick sat across from her dad. The background looked like the cruise Mum had mentioned they had their reception on. Giselle could see food and people around them, all having a great time. On the other page of the album was another photo of her dad with more friends. A little blonde girl sat on his lap, her back towards the camera. She wore a white dress and a daisy wreath on her head. The tiny flower girl made Giselle suddenly feel so alone and nostalgic as a pang of sadness burst through her heart. She touched the photo gently. Her dad looked kind, and she was sure he would have made an amazing father.

Feeling heavyhearted, Giselle drew that photo of her dad with the little girl. A pang of jealousy tore through her. Who was that girl, and why did she get to spend time with her dad and she didn't?

Get a grip, she told herself. Why was she feeling so emotional all of a sudden? She put the pencil down and continued looking through the photos. She saw another one of herself and Nonno when she was around two years old. They were at a park. She could see the swing in the background and some birds flying up high. She leaned closer and realised that it looked just like her dream. The swing, the birds, the park, the ocean; her heart beat fast. As she stared at the photo, she noticed the edge of another photo behind it. Giselle frowned and pulled it out. A loud gasp escaped her lips, and suddenly she couldn't breathe. Staring back at her in the photo was the image of the beautiful blonde lady from the locket. When she flipped the photo to the back, the initials O. A. B. jumped up at her.

Nonno's mistress!

Tears welled in her eyes. She had hoped she was wrong about Nonno's affair with Ophelia, but here she was hidden behind *their* photo. Giselle took a few breaths as tears began to fall.

Oh, Nonno, why?

Chapter 18

Giselle wiped the tears from her eyes and stood up, grabbing the locket from her satchel. She opened the locket and placed it next to the photo she held in her hand. They were the same. It was definitely the same woman.

Then she remembered something she had forgotten. A few times when she had visited her Nonno in his shed, he had been holding this photo and staring at it. Giselle covered her mouth as she recalled one of these days, so many years ago.

Giselle had crawled up onto his lap and stared at the pretty lady with blonde hair.

"Nonno, who's that?"

Nonno had tried to hide the photo, but he was too late.

Giselle took the locket out of his other hand and held it in her little hands. "What's this, Nonno?"

Nonno took it back and said, "It's a treasure, darling. One day when you are grown up, I will tell you all about it." He closed the locket and put it back into the box, which on the outside looked like a book. Then, he placed the photo into his shirt pocket and offered to take her to the park to ride her bike.

"Don't tell your grandmother, okay?" he said.

She looked up at him and asked, "Can I tell Mummy?"

"No, not Mummy either. It's our little secret, okay?"

Ready for their park adventure, she nodded and hopped off his lap to go grab her banana-coloured bike.

Oh, how she wished she had asked him more questions about the locket before he died. At least asked the name of the woman whose picture was in the locket.

With a thumping heart, Giselle began putting the pieces of the puzzle together: Nonno looking at the photo and holding the locket, telling her not to tell Grandmama, calling her Rosie at the nursing home and apologising, and the woman's photo hidden behind another that featured her and Nonno during one of their park trips.

In her mind, all these clues proved he had had an affair. Giselle put the locket back into her bag and stared for several moments at the woman's photo in her hands. She needed to talk to someone. Could she call Jace? No, she didn't know him well enough. Indi. She would call Indi. Quinn was probably busy babysitting those crazy brothers of hers.

Giselle called Indigo. "Hi, Gi," came the voice at the other end.

Giselle melted and tears ran down her cheeks.

"Oh, Gi, what's wrong?" Her friend's concern made Giselle sniffle even more.

Taking a deep breath, she finally spoke. "Indi, I found another photo of that woman from the locket. And I remember Nonno hiding it when I was little," she said in a rush.

She spilled out everything to Indigo, who listened quietly on the other end.

"He had an affair, and I feel completely shattered." Giselle sobbed.

"Gi, I know you don't want to do this, but you need to tell your grandmother. You have to tell her the truth. You'll feel better."

"I can't. I can't tell Grandmama that Nonno had an affair. What would that do to her?" Giselle wiped her tears with her school tie.

A soft sound caught her attention, and when she turned around, her heart leaped to her throat.

"Grandmama," she whispered. She felt the blood drain from her face. One look on her grandma's face told her that she had heard everything. "Got to go," she said to Indi. She hung up the phone and lifted her hand with the photo in it.

"I used to see Nonno looking at this photo when I was little, and I found it today in the albums." Giselle tried to talk louder, but her throat felt like it was being squeezed by steel fingers.

"You think your Nonno had an affair?" Grandmama's tone sent cold chills down Giselle's spine.

Giselle nodded ever so slowly.

Grandmama strode towards Giselle and snatched the photo out of her hand. She stared at the photo in silence. "How dare you doubt your grandfather?" she snapped, then hurried out the door.

Giselle followed close behind. "I love Nonno, and I don't want to believe he had an affair, but all the evidence points to it. It's all there." Her grandmama's little heels click-clacked angrily down the hallway.

"If you loved him, you would never bring up such an accusation, Giselle. Out of all the granddaughters, you were his favourite. He loved all of you, but you were always special to him. He adored you." Her grandmama stopped and stared at her, the photo of the blonde woman still in her hand. "I would appreciate it if you had some respect for him. You obviously did not know him very well." She spun around and dashed upstairs.

Giselle blinked a few times. She felt like she had been slapped. Fighting furious tears, she ran to the living room, grabbed her bag, stormed out of the house, and bolted towards the bus stop. Heavy tears fell onto her school blouse and tie. She looked down and noticed her father's daisy brooch pinned to her tie. She had no father or Nonno with her anymore, and now it looked like she had no Grandmother. More tears spilled down her cheeks. Her face felt stiff from all the crying she had done that afternoon.

A loud honk made her jump, and she turned to look. She saw her grandmama's navy Mercedes-Benz following her. The driver's window rolled down. "Giselle, get in, please. I will not allow you to catch the bus."

Giselle folded her arms across her chest and looked away.

"Get in, please. Don't be stubborn like your mother." Her grandmama's crisp no-nonsense voice made her look her way. There was no use in arguing, so Giselle hoisted her bag on her shoulder and got into the car.

The drive home was awkward. Giselle stole glances at her grandma's translucent statue-like face. Her skin seemed pale, and she looked more fragile than usual. Giselle knew that her grandmama was shocked by news of Nonno's affair but was trying not to show her emotions. Like always.

The drive home seemed to take three hours instead of just thirty minutes. When Grandmama pulled into Uncle Mick's driveway, Giselle could not wait to get out.

"I'm sorry," she whispered and hurried up the dark steps to the front door.

She heard the car drive off.

Giselle leaned her head against the door and sighed. Everything was ruined.

Once inside, she ran up to her room, threw her herself onto her bed, and cried. She was so glad her mum would not be home for another hour.

The ding of her phone surprised her. She blinked a few times, and her eyes felt hot and puffy. The message was from Kim's Café. It was Talia.

HI GISELLE, WOULD YOU BE ABLE TO DO A 6 O'CLOCK SHIFT TOMORROW MORNING? HALEE IS SICK, AND WE NEED SOMEONE DESPERATELY. YOU CAN CHANGE FOR SCHOOL HERE, AND THEN I CAN DROP YOU OFF SO YOU'RE NOT LATE.

Without another thought, she sent the message and crawled into bed.

SURE. I'LL BE THERE.

The panicked squawking of the birds in the sky startled Giselle. She grabbed onto the sides of the swing with all her might and watched them fly away. Big, fat black clouds rolled in overhead as a downpour approached. A flash of lightning zigzagged across the atmosphere. A storm was coming. She glanced sideways and planned her escape. If she followed the long, winding path, she would be able to get away from the storm and the strange woman who had tried to take her so many times. As her brain planned the escape, she felt someone begin to swing her back and forth. Her head spun around and was relieved to see her dad.

He winked at her. "Higher?" he asked.

She shook her head and pointed to the clouds. "I want to go home. There's a storm coming. Please, Daddy, take me home."

Her dad stood facing her in the swing, and he fixed his glasses. "Sweetheart, you are safe with me. Daddy will keep you safe."

"That's right," she heard a strange female voice say. "Your Nonno will look after you."

Giselle frowned. *Nonno?*

When she turned to look for her dad, the man wasn't her dad anymore; he was Nonno. His eyes twinkled and crinkled in the corners. "Liv is right, dear. I will always look after you." He grinned.

Then, behind Nonno, the strange hands with long, thin, manicured nails appeared. When they reached for Giselle, Giselle screamed, "No! No! Don't touch me! I hate you!"

The woman didn't move away; instead, she moved closer. Her long blonde hair cascaded to her waist, and the dragonfly locket dangled from the neck.

Giselle's eyes grew wide, and she gasped. With sudden force, she took hold of the locket and wrenched it off the woman's neck. The woman screamed.

Giselle hurled it towards the ocean. "Go away! Go away!" she yelled over and over again.

The woman's hands and hair became like a hologram, and she puffed away like smoke.

Giselle jerked out of the nightmare. Her heart pounded, and tears streamed down her face. With trembling hands she reached for her lamp and turned it on. The soft peaceful glow of the light illuminated her room and filled her with a small measure of peace.

She got out of bed and grabbed some tissues to wipe her cheeks and nose. Her alarm clock flashed 3:33 a.m. She groaned. Why couldn't morning come sooner?

Giselle went back to bed but didn't turn the light off. She couldn't fall asleep. She played some soft music from her favourite Christian artist and soon fell into a troubled sleep.

The sound of her phone vibrating woke her up. Giselle rubbed her grainy eyes and reached for her phone.

"Hello?" she croaked.

"Finally, you pick up! Why didn't you show up?"

"Talia?" Giselle sat up in her bed. Her eyes glanced at the clock: 9:30 a.m.

"I have been calling you all morning. You were supposed to turn up to your shift three hours ago."

"Oh my gosh, I overslept!" Panic seized her hammering heart. "Talia, I'm so, so sorry! I couldn't sleep last night and then I overslept. My alarm didn't go off." Giselle scrambled off the bed and rushed around her room looking for her bag and school uniform.

On the other end of the phone, Talia was going off on her. Giselle didn't have the energy to listen to her right now.

"Sorry, I have to go. I have to get to school." Giselle hung up and threw the phone across the bed.

Tears of frustration filled her eyes. The fight with Grandmama dashed in her mind, and she winced. Her nightmare and the fact that Kim was probably going to fire her made her dissolve into tears.

She couldn't go to school. Not today. She crawled back into her bed and sent her mum a text.

HEY, MA, I'M FEELING SICK TODAY—I STAYED HOME. GOING BACK TO BED.

Her phone rang seconds after she hit the send button. It was her mum. They talked for a few minutes, and then she hung up to go back to bed.

She couldn't sleep, though—her mind would not shut down. Feeling cranky, Giselle decided to go for a walk around the block. She didn't have the energy to ride her bike to the lighthouse. Today was not a good day.

Chapter 19

After the invigorating long walk around the block, Giselle went to take a shower. When she walked out, she felt more relaxed and at ease. After having a bowl of yoghurt and fruits to eat, she took her artwork to the veranda, put some music on, and began to draw.

"Oh no." She slapped her forehead as the sudden realisation that the draft idea was due today. Her teacher would be upset she was absent today.

Giselle looked through her artwork and decided to take photos with her phone and send what she had sketched so far.

"This dumb phone!" she muttered. The old phone did not take images.

She grabbed her laptop and tried to figure out how to screenshot the images. No luck. She couldn't find the right button, and nothing seemed to work.

"I give up." She groaned. She hated being so technically challenged. Seriously, everyone knew how to use their laptops, but she had always preferred art books to computers.

She wrote her teacher a long email and told her she would have something for her tomorrow.

She sent a quick text to her best friends and another to Sophie, then went back to her art assignment.

A few minutes later, her phone rang. It was Sophie.

Giselle answered it immediately. "Soph, aren't you in class?"

"Relax, it's lunchtime here. I'm in my room. Oh my goodness, what happened?" she asked.

Giselle gave her a brief outline of her morning and her missed work shift.

"I'm so fired, Soph! I can't afford to lose my job. I need the money." Giselle's agitated voice rose a few pitches.

"Have you called Kim to apologise and let her know?" Sophie's questions hung in the air.

Giselle felt her brow crease. "Um, no. Do I need to?" She bit her bottom lip.

"Yes! Tell her before Talia tells her. I mean, maybe she already has, but it'll look really good if you ring her. Trust me, my daddy has taught me a few things about business and dealing with people." Sophie's silvery laugh echoed in Giselle's ear.

"Soph, you are a genius. I'll ring her after I hang up with you." Giselle smiled for the first time that morning.

"Oh, and don't forget to pray before calling. Daddy always says that helps."

The girls said goodbye, and Giselle held her phone near her chest.

Pray? She wondered if she could. She had not even been doing her devotional lately, not to mention the lies she had told her mum. A tinge of guilt washed over her.

Taking a deep breath, she dialled Kim's number and waited three solid rings for her to pick up.

"Giselle, how can I help you?" Kim said.

Giselle cleared her throat, "Um, well. I'm ringing to apologise for missing my shift this morning. I was supposed to cover Halee's shift 'cause she's sick, but I overslept and didn't show up. Talia called me. I'm really sorry, Kim. I didn't sleep well and slept right through my alarm." Giselle's words tumbled into one big mess.

The silence on the other side made her fidget.

Finally, she heard Kim come back to life. "Giselle, first of all, thank you for calling and telling me yourself. I have utter respect that you even called me. Thank you. Secondly, Talia had already told me, but I appreciated it coming directly from you. I was thinking about your job today, but since it was an honest mistake, I will keep you on. I will talk to Talia this afternoon."

Giselle felt her lips stretch into a grin. "Thank you, Kim. Thank you so much."

She hung up and leaned her head on the wall. She closed her eyes as relief flowed through her.

Suddenly, just as she was about to go inside to grab something to eat, the nightmare she'd pushed away tumbled into her head.

She gawked. Oh my goodness, she suddenly remembered something from the dream this time: Nonno had called the woman Liv. Giselle's heart thundered in her chest, and she whispered the name "Liv."

Why had Nonno called her Liv and not Ophelia? Was that his love affair nickname for her? Giselle wrote the name in her book and thought about it for a while. Something about that name bothered her.

What if Ophelia wasn't the one Nonno had had the affair with, and it was someone else? Or what if it was something else completely different?

She tried to clear away these thoughts and went inside to make herself a sandwich. The house's unnerving silence seemed to engulf her today more than ever. She now understood why Uncle Mick barely spent time in his stately mansion.

Once outside on the veranda, she turned the music up and ate her sandwich. She thought about the nightmare, the affair, Nonno, Ophelia, her assignment, Jace, her trip to Europe, and the passport. She had almost forgotten about the passport renewal she needed.

An idea popped into her head. It was hours away before her mum came home. Maybe she could get into the safety box and take out her passport. Uncle Mick has a photocopier in his office, so she could take copies of her passport, then put it back in the safety box. She reasoned that it was the best option. Determined, Giselle put her things away and headed to the office where her mum stored the safety box.

She locked the front door in case her mum turned up suddenly, and tiptoed to the office. She rolled her eyes. She didn't even know why she was tiptoeing—no one was home.

She reached for the door handle and gave it a little tug; it was unlocked. She debated if she should go in or just forget about the whole passport thing.

Ezi's words stumbled back from the other day at the park: *It took six months! So, my advice is for you to get your old passport ASAP!*

Giselle knew Ezi was right. If she got everything in order, she wouldn't have to worry about it anymore.

With her mind made up, Giselle opened the door wide and went in. She closed it gently behind her and turned on the standing lamp. The soft glow filled the room. Giselle moved towards the safety box that looked more like a normal cabinet. She opened the little cream door and came face-to-face with the safe deposit box. It was grey in colour, and it had a dial combination padlock like the ones used on her school's lockers.

Giselle closed the door with a bang. She felt like a cat burglar and couldn't bring herself to try a combination and take the passport.

There must be another way to get a copy of the old passport. She sat on the soft cream carpet for a few minutes but could not think of any other options. "Okay, don't be a wimp and just do it," she said out loud.

She took a big gulp of air, opened the cupboard door again, and started to try out numbers. She used dates that meant something to her mum.

She tried mum's date of birth. Nothing.

She tried her wedding date. Nothing.

She went through Nonno's birthday, Grandmama's, her dad's birthday, but nothing unlocked the door.

Sweat dripped down Giselle's forehead and nose. She hadn't bothered to open the window or turn on the air con. Now she was stifling in the hot, stuffy room. She was about to give up, but another number popped in her head. She frowned. Could it be her birthday?

She shrugged and gave it a try.

Voilà! The lock popped open.

Giselle breathed with relief and wiped the sweat off her face. She leaned down and peered inside. She expected to see jewellery and money, but all she saw was a brown leather folder tucked inside. She reached for it and smiled when she saw the initials W. B. engraved in the corner.

"Warren Bray," she whispered; the folder was her dad's.

Somehow holding the brown case in her hands made her feel close to him.

The folder had a gold button clasp in the centre. She unclasped it, and inside were a few papers and documents. She searched to see if there was a passport for her and found it at the bottom.

She opened it up, but it was her dad's. Flipping through it absentmindedly, she was about to put it back when something caught her attention. She flipped to another page and saw a photo of her as a tiny two-year-old. She touched the photo gently and smiled at how cute she looked. She hurried down the hall towards her uncle's study to take some copies. The door was locked.

"What?! No, no." Giselle tried again, but it was indeed locked.

Feeling deflated, she hurried to put everything back. She would have to wait until Sophie came for the long weekend. She would know where Uncle Mick kept the office key.

Giselle knelt back down and started to put the passport back in its place when her phone rang.

The sudden sound made her jump, and she dropped the papers all over the floor. *Oh no! Giselle, you are such a clutz,* she told herself.

She didn't want to answer her phone. What if whoever it was found out she had broken into the safe? She wasn't that great at hiding her emotions. No, she would call them later. She hurriedly reached for the scattered papers and gently began to put them inside her dad's folder one by one. She could not risk creasing them.

An official-looking piece of paper with a huge logo sat on the top with the words *Birth Certificate* on it.

Giselle gasped; it was *her* birth certificate. Feeling excited and curious, she read her name: Giselle Olivia Bray. There in black and white was her place and date of birth, and underneath was her father's surname and forename, and then it continued with her mother's name. Giselle paused; it said Olivia.

"What? Whoa, the people have messed this up," Giselle said out loud. She was totally engrossed in her birth certificate. "Mum's name is Lousiana." She scanned the rest of the document.

Mother's forename: Olivia Anne.

Giselle laughed. "Okay, so what were these people on when they filled this out?" She turned it over. Maybe this was a sample?

She turned it back and read from the start. Under "Child" it had her name, date, and place of birth. Her dad's name was right, but her mum's wasn't.

Her chest constricted. *What?! No.* She stood up, turned on the main light, and reread the document several times. Her heartbeat accelerated. Who was Olivia Anne Bray? And why was her name written under "Mother"? Giselle shook her head vigorously. Was she in the nightmare?

Chapter 20

Giselle's hand shook. She closed her eyes for a few minutes. This confusion could not be happening to her right now. She rubbed her right temple, took a deep breath, and reread the document. The name of the woman remained the same: *Olivia Anne Bray.*

Feeling sick, she went back to the cupboard, took out all the papers from the folder, and spread them out on the carpet. She had to go through each one. Something did not make sense.

The ding of her phone interrupted her thoughts. Feeling agitated, she decided to turn the phone off so she could concentrate. She went through some of the documents until she came across a marriage certificate. This one had her mum's and dad's names and the date they were married, and attached to it with a paper clip was a photo. Giselle gulped—it was from their wedding day. The photo featured her mum dressed in her boho maxi lace dress with the daisy wreath on her head, her dad in his wedding attire, and a little girl. The girl was about two years old and dressed in a little white dress.

A daisy wreath sat on her blonde hair. The three of them were smiling, and Dad carried her while her mum held the marriage certificate. The little girl she had seen in the photo the other day at Grandmama's house was *her*. Giselle shook her head. How could she be in her parents' wedding when her mum had told her she was born a year later?

There were other papers and another photo with her and her mum at the wedding wearing their wreaths. They were touching nose to nose and laughing. Giselle turned the photo over and written in her mum's writing were the words "Giselle and me on my wedding day. Looking forward to being her mum."

"Being her mum?" Giselle reread the sentence out loud.

Something didn't make sense. She looked at the photo of her mum on her wedding day. It *definitely* was her mother, Lousiana. She read the birth certificate again and paused at the mother's name.

Mother's forename: Olivia Anne.

How could that be? How could the woman in the photo be her mother Lusi, but the mother's name on her birth certificate be someone called Olivia Anne? Was Lusi not her biological Mum?

Giselle rummaged through other papers and stopped at one in particular. The heading stunned her.

Certificate of Adoption.

Giselle let out a cry as the realisation hit her hard: Lousiana was not her birth mum. She was her adoptive mother!

Suddenly, feeling dizzy and sick, she stood up, grabbed her phone, and rushed upstairs to grab her bag. She tripped on the stairs a few times, but she didn't seem to notice. In her room, she grabbed her bag, threw her diary and art book into it, and headed out the door to the garage. She had to leave.

Filled with anguish and anxiety, Giselle mounted her bike and rode to the lighthouse. Tears streamed down her cheeks as she pedalled up the hill and around the corner. When she saw the tall monument come into view, security filled her heart. Not bothering to secure her bike at the bike racks, she dismounted, threw her bike onto the grass, and ran behind the lighthouse to her favourite hidden spot.

Once there, Giselle sobbed. Lousiana wasn't her mum. Her mum was someone else with the name Olivia. She cried even more. She cried for her dead father, her unknown mother—had her birth mum abandoned her? who was she?—she cried because the woman she thought was her mum wasn't. Why had she lied to her? Why hadn't she told her the truth? Giselle shook her head and tried to clear her cottony brain. Her whole life felt like a lie.

The hours went by slowly. The sun was beginning to sink behind the horizon, and a cool gentle breeze began to pick up. It was going to be dark soon, and she did not want to be up there in the darkness. She glanced around and wondered where she could go. Should she ring the twins? Her brow creased. Were they even her cousins anymore? If her mum was not her birth mum, then they weren't her cousins.

Giselle felt like a dagger was being stabbed into her heart, and she began to cry again. Uncontrollable sobs tore through her body. She cried until her tears dried up and exhaustion took over. Soft darkness began to envelop her, and she could no longer see the water below. Strange shadows danced from different corners. Feeling afraid, Giselle thought for a minute about who she could call.

Jace.

Her fingers trembled as she took her phone out of her bag, unlocked it and looked for Jace's number. She ignored the missed calls and voice messages that flashed on her screen. She couldn't deal with them right now. Through her tears, she texted him.

ARE YOU STILL WORKING? CAN I CALL YOU?

She had just pressed send when his call came through.

"Hey, Giselle. I just finished my shift. You okay?" Jace's cheery voice came through the other end. He was oblivious to her pain.

"Could you do me a huge favour, please?" She tried to control the shakiness in her voice but knew it was hopeless.

"Are you hurt?' he asked, his voice filled with concern.

Giselle ignored his question. "Could you drop me off at my grandmother's, please?"

"Sure! I'll come to your house now." She could hear Jace zip up a bag.

"I'm not there. I'm at the lighthouse. I'm not hurt. I just need my grandma. Please don't ask me any questions,

Jace. I can't talk about it yet." Her voice shook, and tears fell down her cheek.

After she hung up, she made her way towards the entry of the lighthouse and waited for Jace. Her eyes darted back and forth, intensely alert, in case she saw someone coming towards her. She had never been at the lighthouse this late before.

It wasn't long before she heard the roar of a motorbike and then saw Jace's bike come round the bend. She exhaled and waved at him.

He didn't say anything. Instead, he got off and engulfed her in a big hug. Her heart ached, and she sobbed into his jacket.

Soon, they were off towards Crest Pointe. Giselle reached her arms around Jace, buried her face into his jacket, and closed her eyes. His soothing presence filled her with a sense of protection and safety.

This time she didn't bother to tell him to drop her off at the corner. She let him drive her down the driveway of Nonno's beloved villa—the villa he had built.

She dismounted from the bike, took off her helmet, and handed it to Jace, "Thank you for dropping me off and thank you for not asking questions." She tried to smile.

He reached for her hand and gave it a squeeze. "Talk to me when you're ready." She leaned in and gave him another hug.

"I saw you left your bike at the lighthouse. I'll get it home for you," he said.

Giselle's eyes filled with tears. How could he be so thoughtful?

She stood outside and watched Jace ride off. She wrang her hands. Would her grandma want to talk to her? After the argument they'd had earlier that week, she wasn't sure. But she needed a place to stay, a place to figure things out. Just then, the outside light turned on, and Grandmama's door opened. "Giselle, darling, I heard a bike?" Her grandmama stuck her head out to see if anyone else was with her.

"I'm alone," she whimpered as tears cascaded down her cheeks again.

Her grandmama reached out, and Giselle ran into her embrace. Tears had wet her neck and shirt. The sudden ringing of her phone startled Giselle. She pulled away and took it out of her bag. It was Mum.

Her heart iced over, and she stretched it out to Grandmama, "I can't talk to *her*."

With a frown on her face, her grandmama reached for the phone and answered it. "Lousiana?" With an eyebrow lifted, her grandmother stared at Giselle. Giselle could hear her mother's agitated voice on the other end. She watched her grandma's face pale and an *O* form on her lips. She stared at Giselle, and tears filled her eyes.

"No, Lousiana, that's not a good idea right now. I will look after Giselle until she's ready to go back to you."

More words were spoken between Grandmama and Lousiana, and after a quick goodbye she hung up and handed Giselle the phone.

"Come in, darling." She ushered Giselle inside and headed to the family room. Giselle followed close behind.

"Get comfortable. I will make some chamomile tea. That always helped your nerves and nightmares when you were a little girl." Her grandmama touched her face gently.

"I'm sorry about yesterday and Nonno," Giselle whispered.

Grandmama shook her head, "Darling, it's already forgotten. Get comfortable and try to relax." She hurried out of the room and left Giselle to her thoughts.

Giselle leaned her head against the sofa and sighed; she had no more tears left to cry. The last few hours had been horrendous. While she waited for the tea, she scrolled through her phone to see who had called her earlier, when she had dropped all her papers. The missed calls and messages were all from Talia. Giselle listened to the first voice message.

"Giselle, could you finish a bit later tonight, please? Halee is still sick, and I need someone to help me close. Call me ASAP."

Giselle gaped. It was Tuesday. She had a shift on Tuesdays, and she had completely forgotten. Oh no. She was so fired. She groaned and threw her phone onto the seat next to her. Frustration and anger filled her heart. How could her so-called mother have done this to her? All the years of lies!

The sound of her grandmother's footsteps made her take a deep breath and bury her anger for now.

"Here you go, darling, chamomile tea." Her grandmama waited for Giselle to sit up. "It has a touch of fresh mint too." She winked.

Giselle smiled softly and thanked her. She sipped away at her tea slowly. She felt trapped in her own sorrow and pain. How she wished Nonno was alive. He always knew what to do and say.

Her grandmama had taken a seat across from her to give her some space. Giselle could tell she wanted to talk. She looked at her and said, "It's delicious."

Her grandma cleared her throat. "Darling, your mother loves you."

Giselle looked away; that was such a lie. If you love someone, you don't lie to them. Someone who loves always tells the truth. Giselle felt cheated and robbed. Who was she really?

"I feel like an idiot!" she spat out.

"Oh, darling, no. No." Her grandmama rushed to her side and took the cup of tea off her hands before she grabbed them in her mature slender ones. "You are not an idiot."

"How could I not see the signs? I mean, she only has photos of me when I'm two. No baby pictures. No pictures of her pregnant with me. Now, it makes sense. I don't want to see her again! I hate her." Tears streamed down Giselle's cheeks, and she sobbed again. Her heart ached. She loved her mother. But if she said she hated her over and over, she would soon truly hate her.

Grandmama let out a sigh and shook her head. "Giselle, you are being harsh on her."

Giselle pulled her hands away. "But she lied to me!"

"No, darling, she protected you!" her grandmama cried.

"Protected me from what? I think she protected herself!" Giselle wiped her eyes and rubbed her sore head. "She should have told me she adopted me."

"Giselle, darling, I think I should tell you everything in detail. I know Lousiana has made some mistakes in life, but raising you as her own was the best thing that ever happened to her. She has adored you from the moment she met you." Her grandmama pressed her lips together.

Giselle closed her eyes for a few seconds and nodded for her grandmama to continue.

"I need to show you something. Go to your old room and change into your pyjamas. I'll meet you back here." Her grandmama tried to smile.

Reluctantly, Giselle headed to the room to change into the floral-print pants she kept there. She put on a cotton top and socks. She went to the bathroom, brushed her teeth, washed her face, and tied her hair into a plait.

When she got back, her grandmama had also changed into her cream silk pyjamas and white slippers. On her lap she had a small wooden box with a white rose design on top. When she saw Giselle, she moved over and patted the seat so she could sit next to her.

"I have some letters and photos I want to show you. I have kept them all these years. They are from your mum, Lusi. When she married your dad, she decided to document every single moment with you. She also wrote letters to Nonno and I about you. I want to read you bits and pieces." Her grandmama opened the box, and Giselle wasn't sure she wanted to hear what the letters said.

Chapter 21

Inside the box Giselle could see folded papers, envelopes, and photos. She frowned as she watched her grandmama pull out an envelope, open it up, and begin reading to her.

"My little Giselle called me Mama for the very first time today. You have no idea how my heart almost burst. I sat in the corner of my bed and cried. I told her to call me Aunty Lusi, but she kept shaking her head saying no and ran around saying, 'Mama, Mama!' I told Warren that night when he got home. He laughed and told me just to let her call me Mama. He said I was the only mother she would know anyway."

Giselle glanced away and stared at the wall. Why had that letter not made her feel any better? When her grandmama reached for another one, she gulped. "Grandmama, can we not read these tonight, please? I want to go to bed." She swallowed; a thick lump had formed in her throat.

"I'm sorry, darling. I should have realised this is too much for you right now. We can talk tomorrow." She leaned over and gave Giselle's shoulders a little squeeze. "Good night, darling."

Giselle stood up and whispered, "Good night and thank you." In slow motion she headed upstairs to her room; her brain felt like it had been stuffed with scrunched-up tissue paper—her head ached, her eyes hurt, and her heart bled.

She crawled into bed and pulled the covers up to her chin. Tonight the shadows in the room bothered her. Thoughts plagued her mind as she wondered what had happened to her birth mother Olivia Anne. Had she left her father and her? Had they divorced? Had she died?

Feeling utterly drained, Giselle closed her eyes and went to sleep.

"Push me higher, Daddy. I want to fly." Her giggles echoed all around her. She felt happy and free. She turned around to see her dad's face, but instead she came face-to-face with the strange woman. She was swinging her higher than she'd ever been.

"No, no, go away!" Giselle screamed as she tried to unbuckle the belt securely holding her in place.

The woman's playful laugh echoed around her. "You can't run away from me, Giselle."

Giselle gasped.

Thunder cracked.

Giselle jumped and stared at the blackened sky. The clouds moved ferociously across the sky. Pelts of rain began to drop, sharp and painful like needles on her skin.

"Daddy, help me!" Giselle shouted as she darted her eyes back and forth.

The woman appeared in front of her. "Giselle, you can't run away from me." Her long blonde hair moved with the wind. The locket was secured on her neck. Giselle lifted her hand and grabbed the locket. The woman pulled back, but Giselle pulled harder.

A sudden clap of thunder reverberated across the sky.

Giselle screamed and woke up. Her heart pounded, and she struggled to breathe. She sat up on her bed shuddering. New tears ran down her cheeks. She hated these nightmares, she hated storms, she hated that her Nonno was dead, and she hated that her mum Lusi, wasn't her mum. She hated life.

By the time she fell asleep again, it was almost dawn.

The loud knock on her door woke her up with a start. Where was she? When her eyes focused on her surroundings, she gulped and sat up. Slowly the previous night's recollections rushed back. She was in her old room at Grandma's.

The knock at the door came again. "Come in," she croaked.

The door opened, and her grandmama's head appeared. "Morning, darling. Sorry to wake you. I just wanted to check that you are okay." Her face looked pale.

Giselle rubbed her eyes and nodded, "What's the time?" she asked.

"It's 11:45."

Her eyes opened wide. "What?! Oh my goodness, I missed school again." She moaned.

165

"It's okay. Your mum rang them and told them you were sick. Would you like to eat something?" Her grandma winked. "I made your favourite."

Giselle lifted an eyebrow.

"Cinnamon rolls straight out of the oven."

Giselle smiled. "Oh yes, please. I'll go shower first and head downstairs soon."

After the door closed, she reached for her phone and saw several missed calls from her mum and text messages from the twins, Sophie, Jace, Indi, and Quinn. Giselle grumbled and curled up in bed again. She did not want to face the day.

In the distance she heard the sound of light thunder. She hopped out of bed and opened the blinds. It was dark outside. Black clouds gathered in the middle of the sky.

She bit her bottom lip and decided to shower straight away. She wanted to be with Grandmama when the storm hit.

After an extra-long warm shower, Giselle changed into a flowing, floral maxi dress and sandals. She was relieved she kept a lot of clothes at Grandmama's house.

She smelled the slightly fruity, peppery, spicy smell of the cinnamon. Her stomach growled. She was starved.

Her grandmama wasn't in the kitchen, but there was a note near a plate with two cinnamon rolls and a cup of steamy peppermint tea sitting next to it.

"Gone to the shops to grab some veggies for our dinner. I'll be back as soon as I am done."

Giselle shivered slightly and turned her head towards the window. The black clouds lingered. Her stomach growled again. She sat on the stool and ate her rolls in sad silence as the roll of thunder echoed in the distance.

At least that's not too close, Giselle thought to herself as she took a sip of her mint tea. The warmth of the food and the tea seemed to calm her.

She looked around the kitchen and sighed. She had so many great memories from when Nonno was alive. If only she could travel back in time and he could make everything better.

The sound of her phone's ring bumped her out of her sweet memories. She checked who it was.

Her heart tumbled. "Jace!" she answered.

"Hey, Giselle. Just wanted to check how you're doing." His light, cheery voice washed over her.

"I've got a headache, and I missed school, again, but I'm all right," she said. "You?"

"I'm great! I have a day off tomorrow. Want to hang out?" He sounded eager.

She bit her bottom lip. "I'm supposed to be sick and away from school. I don't want them to think I'm lying."

"We could go to the lighthouse for a picnic. I'll get the food from Kim's." She could hear his voice smile.

At the mention of Kim's name, Giselle groaned. She didn't want to think about the Café, Talia or the shifts she has missed. She felt awful not answering their calls. But, at this moment it was impossible for her to call them back and explain the situation.

"Or we could go to the Mexican place we went last time. I'll go anywhere you want. I just want to see you." She could hear his voice soften.

Her heart melted. "Okay, pick me up at ten at the corner near the bus stop. I don't want Grandma to see you and totally freak out."

After they said goodbye, she drank the last of the tea and noticed that the heavy clouds had lifted. Relief washed over her. After washing her dirty plate and mug, Giselle went to her room to write and draw in her diary. This was the best way she could process her thoughts.

Dear Diary,

The last day has been a nightmare. I wish I could turn back time and forget everything. I wish I had never sneaked into the safe and found out those secrets. All because of my stupid passport. Why did I have to stress so much about the passport? Why did I listen to Ezi anyways? Since when is she an authority on the government? I'm so mad at her! Wait, I need to chill. It's not Ezi's fault. I'm just being mean and ugly. I hate feeling so confused and twisted inside my heart. I don't know what to do. I don't know what I'll do if ~~my mum~~ she turns up here today or tomorrow. I don't want to see her. I hate her! I hate that she married Daddy. I hate that she adopted me.

Giselle stopped writing and threw her pen onto the bed; she could not write another word. The sadness that engulfed her felt suffocating. She stood up and decided to draw instead, or maybe she should reply to the text messages. Giselle cringed when she saw that she had a voice message from Kim. Again. She was probably 100 percent fired. She smiled inside at the concern in Quinn's and Indi's texts and replied that she was sick and taking some days off school. The twins texted and asked why she was away. She replied the same. She didn't want to get into the details. The last text was Sophie's, but Giselle dreaded opening it. Reluctantly, she read it: GI, CALL ME!!!!

Just before texting back she heard the sound of the door open downstairs, indicating that her grandmama was home. Maybe she should help her make dinner. Giselle loved to cook and found being in the kitchen very relaxing.

Giselle shook her head and texted Sophie back. SORRY, SOPH, CAN'T RIGHT NOW. ABOUT TO COOK DINNER WITH GRANDMAMA. WILL CALL YOU LATER. XO.

She could not deal with Soph right now. Making dinner was sounding more like a good idea. Before putting her phone down on her bed, she deleted her mum's six missed calls.

She hurried downstairs and saw her grandmother busy in the kitchen beginning the dinner preparations. Her calm, elegant presence filled Giselle's heart with peace. In the background a soft Italian folk song played. Nonno's favourite.

"Hi, darling, how are you feeling?" Her grandmama looked up from the sink where she was washing some zucchinis.

Suddenly feeling overwhelmed with emotions, Giselle hurried over to her grandmama and hugged her tight.

"Thank you for having me here and for not sending me away to my . . . to her." She pursed her lips.

Grandmama turned off the tap and disentangled herself from Giselle's embrace. She grabbed her hand in her crinkly wet ones. "Oh, my beautiful Giselle. I would never send you away. Having you here has felt like old times. Do you remember the fun we had in this kitchen cooking up a storm?"

Giselle wiped her eyes and grinned. "And Nonno stealing cookies and pretending he hadn't."

"But his shirt was covered in crumbs." Grandmama burst out laughing, as did Giselle.

She could still see his cheeky face pretending to be innocent.

A realisation hit her. "Do you think Nonno would be mad at me right now?" she asked softly.

"Mad at you?" Grandmama's brow wrinkled.

"Well, because I'm so angry at *her*."

Grandmama dried her hands on the blue-and-white tartan dishcloth. "He wouldn't be angry. Just disappointed. Remember, darling, for him family was everything. He would be devastated if he knew you were not speaking at each other, but never angry. That's just the way he was."

Giselle nodded slowly and reached for the cloth to dry her damp hands. She knew Grandmama was right. But she couldn't bring herself to forgive *her*.

The beauty of a sunny day greeted Giselle early the next morning. She decided to go for a long walk around the neighbourhood and clear her head. She felt a little better this morning, and butterflies danced in her stomach as she thought of Jace coming to pick her up.

She had told Grandmama last night that she was meeting up with a friend because she needed to chat and clear her head. Grandmama had offered to drop her off, but she said she would be fine and it would be good for her to get distracted.

A few minutes before ten, she saw Jace come towards the bus stop area. Her heart fluttered and she immediately grinned.

"Hey." His eyes and voice softened when he looked at her. "It's good to see you."

She beamed. "It's good to see you too!"

He winked. "Hop on."

She smiled and jumped on the back of his bike. The accelerated ride and her arms around Jace made Giselle forget the drama she had experienced the last couple of days. With him she felt safe.

The weather was so delightful that Giselle wanted to dive into the cool waters below. She turned to help Jace unpack their picnic lunch and set up a blanket. While they set up, she thanked him for taking her bike back home for her. He shrugged and said it was totally okay.

They had just sat down to eat when the ring of her phone startled her. She checked it and saw Sophie was calling. "Oh no!" she said. She had completely forgotten to call her back. She put her phone on silent and gave her total attention to Jace.

"By the way," she began, "how old are you anyways? I mean, you act more mature than the weird guys in my class, so I'm guessing you're older than seventeen?" She tilted her head and narrowed her hazel eyes.

Jace's green eyes sparkled. "Take a guess," he challenged as he moved his face from side to side posing like a model about to have his photo taken.

Giselle laughed. "I'm guessing . . . um, thirty-five."

His eyes widened. "No way. I can't look that old. Can I?" He grabbed his phone and looked at his reflection.

Giselle hit his arm. "I'm just teasing." She giggled. Her hand lingered on his strong arm. She cleared her throat. "Okay, but seriously."

"I'm nineteen," he said as he took a bite of his turkey sandwich.

Giselle grinned. "You look nineteen," she said. She also wanted to add *and you are super cute and have a hot body.* She blushed and looked away. *Stop it,* she told herself.

"Your phone's ringing." Jace pointed to her phone on the blanket. She could see the light flashing. It was Sophie again.

"It could be important," Jace added.

Giselle shook her head and decided to tell him everything that had happened in the last twenty-four hours.

Chapter 22

Dear Diary,

It felt sooo good to have talked to Jace about everything that's happened—he is totally a good listener, and he didn't try to defend ~~my mum~~ her or anything. He just listened and took my hand in his, which felt totally weird. I mean, my stomach kept doing funny somersaults each time he touched me. Am I being dumb?

Anyways, I felt so much better after talking to him, and then he told me I had to ring Soph when I got home. I knew he was right. When Jace dropped me off, I saw him lean in as if he was going to kiss me. I watched him lean closer and closer, and he kept staring at my lips. I think I almost had a coronary right then and there, but just as he got closer, the bus honked for him to move his bike. We were on the wrong stop place. Anyways, he didn't kiss me after all, and I think that's okay. I don't know if I wanted him to kiss me or not. I mean, I think I did. I like him lots, but I think my brain isn't there right now. I'm so confused, and there's way too much going on in my life.

Anyways, when I got to Grandmama's, I called Soph. When she picked up the phone, she cried, and then I started to cry.

Seriously, it felt like we were eighty-year-old grandmas crying, LOL. Finally, when we stopped our sobbing, she talked.

"Daddy told me everything!" Sophie whimpered. "Aunt Lusi called him and told him that you found out she isn't your birth mum. Then he called me so I could check in on you. Gi, I almost passed out. I have been crying each time I think of it!"

Then she was silent. I totally freaked out. I braced myself for what she was going to say next.

"You're still my Hayes sister," she told me.

My heart almost burst and I bawled. My biggest fear was losing my cousins. My best friends and the people I loved most in the entire world.

We told each other we'll love each other forever.

I could barely talk. I honestly have cried more in the last few days than in my entire life. Sophie said she's coming home this weekend for the public holiday. She said she has to see me and wishes I was back home. But I told her I can't, not with my . . . not with her there. Then she said she'd stay at Grandmama's, too, on Friday night; that way we can talk. I was relieved and excited. I have to see Soph. I can't wait. After hanging up, I headed downstairs and helped Grandmama make dinner. She asked me if I was ready to see more photos and letters. I really didn't want to. What for? All these years, she completely lied and never told me I had another mum somewhere. I took a deep breath and asked Grandmama if she knew what had happened to my birth mum. Grandmama nodded and said my mum passed away when I was little.

She passed away. I suddenly felt empty.

I nodded and didn't say a word. There was nothing to say. Back in my room, I texted Soph and told her what I'd found out. She texted back: WE BOTH DON'T HAVE MUMS.

At least she had a dad. I was truly an orphan.
An orphan!

Giselle stopped writing and gasped. The word *orphan* seemed to jump off the page at her as if in neon giant letters. Tears filled her eyes; she was an orphan. She didn't have a mum or a dad. She was alone in this world. Giselle buried her face in her pillow and cried herself to sleep.

The sound of the doorbell chime woke her up with a start. For a second she thought she was dreaming, until she heard footsteps heading downstairs. Someone was here. Giselle groaned and turned over on the bed. She wanted to go back to sleep.

A soft knock on her door interrupted any thoughts she had about going back to sleep. "Come in." She sat up and tied her hair into a low ponytail. She checked her phone; it was eight o'clock.

The door opened, and Giselle gasped. It was her mother.

"You're not answering any of my calls. I had to come and see you." Her mum walked into the room carrying a leopard-print tote bag.

Giselle tried to look away, but she was shocked at seeing her mum so disheveled. Her unwashed blonde hair was loosely tucked behind her ears, her black singlet and jeans looked like they had not seen an iron in centuries, and she had zero makeup on to hide the black circles under her eyes. Giselle cringed. She looked horrendous.

"We need to talk. I know I messed up, honey, but I need to tell you what happened." Her mum moved towards the bed.

Giselle turned her face away and looked out the window. "I don't want to talk about it, and I don't want to talk to *you*." She choked out the last words and tried hard not to cry

The silence in the room intensified until Giselle felt like she was being strangled.

"You have every right to be mad. I just—"

"Please go away." Giselle closed her eyes as tears rolled down her cheeks.

More silence.

She turned as her mum headed back out the door, but she stopped and turned back. "This was left for you. It's time you had it." She placed the tote bag onto the bed and left the room. Her shoulders hunched and her head bowed.

Giselle hit the bed with her fist as anger bubbled up inside. A part of her wished she hadn't treated her so badly, but she also figured, well, she deserved it. Her eyes travelled to the tote bag, and for a second she considered throwing it into the bin. She shook her head. She needed at least to peek inside. Slowly she opened it, and sitting at the bottom was a leather journal with a note on top. Giselle picked up the piece of paper and gasped when she read it.

To: Giselle

From: Olivia Anne Bray

Olivia Anne was the name she had seen on her birth certificate. Her birth Mother.

With unsteady hands, Giselle picked up the journal and touched the engraved dragonfly on the front cover.

"Mum!" she exhaled.

Giselle opened the first page, where there was a message addressed to her! She began to read.

Dear Giselle,

Oh, my darling girl, if you are reading this, you must be a teenager giving your dad grey hair. That's the job of every teenager, right? :)

You might be wondering who I am—well, let me introduce myself. My name is Olivia Anne Bray, formerly known as Olivia Anne Dawson before marrying your father. I am your mother. I was born in Ashford a town in Kent. Your dad and I have been married for eight years. I thought I couldn't have babies and never would. We have waited a long time for you. But a year ago you made your arrival in Bristol, where we now live. Oh, the joy you've brought to me and your father. We adore you, my love, and by the looks of things, I think you adore us too. You are one year old, and you're already walking around, giving your father grief. Ha ha ha. He worries that you might fall and hurt yourself, but I assure him that if that happens, you will be okay. You will stand up and keep walking. Of course, he doesn't believe me, for he is a bit overprotective. You are Daddy's little girl, for sure.

Darling, six months ago I was diagnosed with cancer. Terminal cancer. Yes, I will die from this cancer. There are days I have hope that I will be okay and be healed, but I know I must be realistic and accept the truth. That's why I have made this journal. It's dedicated to you, my little Giselle. Inside you will find photos of me pregnant with you, wedding photos of your father and me, our trips, our home, days at the ocean, and several other memories. I hope you get to know me through these pages, and you enjoy my images. Almost all the images were taken by me. I love photography and dreamed of one day having a studio. Your dad is an amazing artist, and I know he will do wonderful things in life. Please take care of him for me, my darling. Look after him when I am gone. Love and accept the woman he marries one day because I have made him promise that he will remarry so he can give you a mum. Someone to love and look after you and him. Your dad needs someone. I'm praying God brings him a great woman. I know He will!

I love you, Giselle, and I hope you get to love a little bit of me in these pages. Know that you were greatly loved by me.

Till we meet in heaven, my love.

Mum xx

Giselle let out a cry and shut the book with a thud. Her breathing came in short and fast breaths, and her heart pounded right through to her temples. She closed her eyes and began to breathe slowly. *Calm down, calm down,* she kept telling herself. Then she took a long shivering breath and opened the book again.

She turned the second page, and her mouth gaped. There in the inside cover of the book was a photo of a blonde woman with the initials O.A.B under it.

"Olivia Anne Bray! Oh my goodness, the locket!" Giselle scrambled out of bed and ran to her bag. She fumbled until she got it open and found the locket.

She opened the locket and put it next to the photo. The pictures were a perfect match.

Giselle touched the face of the woman in the photo and touched the face of the baby. It was her as a baby and her mum.

"Oh Nonno," she whispered. "I'm so sorry." How could she have thought that Nonno would have an affair! He didn't have an affair; he had been holding her treasure all these years. She had to apologise to Grandmama.

"Giselle?"

At the sound of her grandmama's voice Giselle looked up with tears in her eyes. "It's my mum," she whimpered.

Her grandmama hurried into the room and engulfed her granddaughter into a long hug. No words were spoken.

She finally wiped her eyes. "Are you okay if I stay in my room today? I just want to read her journal."

Her grandmama nodded. "Of course. I will bring you something to eat."

Giselle nodded and went back to bed to read all about her mum. With each page, she found out something new. She laughed at her dad's funny photos and was captivated by the photos of herself as a baby. This was the first time she was seeing photos of herself as a newborn. Her heart swelled.

Feeling emotionally and physically tired, Giselle put the book away and decided to go back to sleep. Her heavy eyes fluttered, and soon she fell asleep thinking of her mum and dad and her life as a baby.

The day was a little overcast. Giselle could see the ocean farther down the park and large birds flying high above as they migrated to a warmer climate. The air smelled like salt, fish, and hot chips, all mingled into one bewildering aroma.

Little butterflies danced in the pit of her stomach as she swung high in the air. Laughter echoed all around her.

"Higher, Daddy! Higher, Daddy!" she squealed.

Her father grinned behind his handsome bearded face. He pushed her with one hand and fixed his glasses with the other. "You're flying, darling. You're flying with the birds." He laughed.

Just as Giselle was about to open her mouth, strange female hands reached out to grab her. Giselle gasped and twisted in her swing as the hands grabbed her by the waist. "Come, darling, it's time to have lunch," the soft voice said. The woman leaned over.

Blonde hair, the locket, and the woman's face came into view.

"Mum!" Giselle gasped.

"Come, darling. Let's eat." The blonde woman from the photo leaned over and gave her a big kiss on her head.

Giselle stretched out her arms and grabbed her mum by the neck. "Mummy, stay here with me. Stay with me."

Her mother laughed. "Oh, darling, of course I'll stay with you. But let me go get the food for you. I will be back." Her mother turned to walk away.

"Don't go, Mum! Don't leave me!" Giselle shouted as she grabbed the woman's dress. "Don't leave me!" she screamed.

Giselle woke up with a start. Her heart pounded.

She sat up on the bed and saw that it was dark, and soft rain pelted gently on the window. She opened her phone and saw missed calls from Kim, Talia, Quinn, and Indi. It was way past midnight, too late to call them back. Besides, she had no energy to talk to anyone. Well, maybe she could text her friends in the morning and talk to them over the weekend. Not wanting to go back to sleep, she grabbed her mother's journal and began to read each treasured page.

Chapter 23

Early the next morning, Giselle woke up with a growling stomach. She had eaten very little the day before. All she wanted today was to sink her teeth into a baguette stuffed with creamy cheese and vegan ham.

As she left her bed, she realised that her mood seemed lighter than it had the last few days. She hurried to shower and dress. Thirty-five minutes later, she ran down the stairs with her mum's journal tucked safely under her arm. She wanted to share with Grandmama a few of the photos and letters she had read the night before.

As Giselle came around the corner, she almost collided with her grandma.

"Oops, sorry!" she said as she came to a screeching halt.

"Uh, darling. What's the hurry?" Grandmama carried a woven basket filled with herbs and lettuce from her vegetable garden. She moved her basket to one side and lifted her cheek for Giselle to kiss it.

Giselle beamed and gave her a tiny peck. "I was super excited to show you my mum's journal. She sounds wonderful!"

She noticed her grandmama's grey-green eyes flicker. "Did you sleep well?" she asked.

Giselle nodded and followed her to the kitchen. "I slept better than any other night recently. I mean, I dreamed about my mum. I couldn't sleep, so I read her journal and eventually I fell asleep. I slept sooo good."

Grandmama placed the basket on her marble bench and said, "I'm glad, darling."

Giselle sat on the bar stool and placed the journal on the counter. She watched as her grandmama washed the herbs and vegetables in the sink. "By the way," she began, "I wanted to apologise again for thinking Nonno had an affair. I know Nonno would never! But I guess everything was so confusing, I didn't know what to think."

"Darling, no need to apologise at all." Grandmama paused as she washed the coriander. "Your grandfather always said that one day he would tell you everything. Lusi was so afraid to do so. But he said he would do it."

Giselle remained silent. She was absorbed in everything her grandmama was saying.

"I often told him to hide that locket and photo before you found out. But he was stubborn and didn't listen to me." She shook her head.

Giselle nodded. "I remember him looking at them. But I didn't know what they were. You know, I miss him every day."

Grandmama's eyes watered. "Me too," she whispered, then cleared her throat. "How about we get breakfast done. I think something delicious is in order." Grandmama dried her hands. "Omelette?"

Giselle closed her eyes. "Mmm, yes, please." She got up to set the table while Grandmama got the eggs ready.

Giselle bit her bottom lip as she thought about school and everything she was missing in her senior year. She hoped next week she was well enough to make an appearance. Besides, she missed her friends.

During breakfast Giselle talked nonstop about her mum and dad, about the journal, the locket, and England. Now more than ever, she wanted to go to Europe and see her parents' graves.

Grandmama listened politely. Then she squeezed her hand. "I am so happy you know the truth about your birth mother, Olivia. Not being able to tell you the truth has bothered me for years." Grandmama's eyes travelled to a big family photo that hung on the dining room wall. "Just don't forget that God blessed you with two mothers. Olivia and my daughter Lusi." With that she patted her hand and began to clear the table.

Giselle's eyes blinked. Her throat tightened. She glanced at the family photo. Her eyes travelled to her Nonno and Grandmama and to her aunts Miriam, Jackeline, and Yasmin. She paused at Uncle Mick's face and slowly stared at the smiling face of her mother. She swallowed and her eyes filled with tears. With a swift movement, she stood up and hurried to help Grandmama clean the kitchen.

The morning seemed to drag on forever. Giselle decided to sit outside with her sketchbook, her mum's journal, and the locket around her neck. As she flipped through yet another page, she paused at a photo and drew in her breath.

In the photo she was about one year old. She was sitting on a swing; her dad pushed her. In the background she could see the ocean and birds flying above. There was another photo of her mum reaching for her. Her long blonde hair flowed freely, and the locket dangled from her neck.

The photo was exactly like the nightmare she had been having. Except Nonno wasn't in it and neither was the storm. Giselle frowned. Why then had they been in her dream? What did they have in common?

The ring of her phone interrupted her thoughts. It was Indi. Giselle picked up and squealed when she answered. Oh, how she missed her friends. They talked for ten minutes, and Giselle promised she would talk to her and Quinn on Sunday afternoon. The events of the past few days were too much to talk about over the phone.

For the rest of the afternoon, Giselle sat outside listening to the sound of the birds and reminiscing about Nonno and her sitting out there trying to name the birds they spotted. Just as she mused over this memory, an idea popped into her head. With her heart pounding, she grabbed her art book and began to sketch her art assignment. She knew exactly what she would draw.

She was so engrossed in her drawing that she did not hear the footsteps coming down the pathway.

"Giselle?" The soft voice of Kiki made her head snap up in surprise.

Giselle turned her head and was shocked to see her four cousins standing there. The twins along with Esmeralda and Silver.

"Oh my goodness, you guys." Giselle stood and rushed to hug them.

Giggles, kisses, and laughter filled the air.

"What happened? What are you guys doing here?" Giselle's words spilled one over the other. "Why aren't you at school?"

Silver was the first one to talk. Her ginger hair looked lovely in a long braid. "We found out what happened, and we had to see you." She looked at the others.

Everyone nodded.

"Hey, can we sit?" Ezi asked, pointing to the garden chairs.

Giselle nodded, and soon they all pulled some of the garden chairs over and sat in a small circle. Giselle shook her head. She had not expected to see her beautiful cousins at all today.

"I found out about you and Aunt Lusi," Emily started. "The other day she rang Mum and was bawling over the phone. Mum had her on speaker. I heard everything." Emily shook her long ponytail. "I actually cried."

"Me too." Kiki piped up, her eyes misted over. She pushed her glasses to the top of her head. "It wasn't Emily who told me for once."

Giselle smiled.

"I found out the same way," Silver said. "Aunt Lusi called Aunty Miriam, and I heard everything. I was horrified, and I rang Ezi and told her over the phone."

"And I could have crashed! I was driving and the shock was intense." Esmeralda shook her massive curls and wiped the corners of her red lips. "I almost had a heart attack. Oh man, Giselle. Talk about a skeleton in the closet!"

"Ezi!" Kiki cried and hit Esmeralda on the leg.

"What?" Oblivious to her words, Esmeralda looked around at the girls.

Kiki rolled her eyes. "The reason we are here is because we want you to know you are still our cousin no matter what!"

Everyone echoed the same thing.

Giselle took a deep breath. "My biggest fear was you guys wouldn't want to be my cousins anymore."

"But why?" Kiki frowned.

"Well, your mums are all sisters. And Uncle Mick is their brother," Giselle stated.

"But, your mum is our mums' sister too." Silver giggled.

"And Uncle Mick's twin," Emily added.

"Yes, I know all that. But my mum is only *my mum* through adoption. We don't share any bloodline whatsoever." Giselle paused and felt her eyes fill with tears.

"We don't care about any of that!" Esmeralda exclaimed. "You are our cousin and that's that!"

Everyone agreed. Soon the girls stood in a circle crying and giggling all at once.

Giselle's heart melted, and she cried with joy. She had been terrified that she could lose her cousins. Afraid they would not see her like one of them because she didn't carry their blood. Relief filled her heart. At the back of her mind, she could hear a little voice saying, *You should accept* her *too.*

But right now she couldn't. She didn't know how.

Her cousins didn't stay long, as they had schoolwork to get done. They just wanted Giselle to know they loved and supported her.

Giselle stood outside and waved goodbye as each car disappeared down the long driveway. Once they were gone, she sighed and went to grab her art book and go inside to the family room. She could hear her grandmama pottering in the kitchen. Having someone at home made her feel less alone. She realised that she loved company. Maybe she should move in with Grandmama. The thought swirled in her head, but could she leave her mum for good? Giselle pursed her lips. She'd rather not go there. She quickly packed up her things and went indoors.

A few hours later, Giselle was so engrossed in her art drawing that the sound of her phone ringing made her jump. It was Uncle Mick.

"Uncle Mick, hi!" Giselle was thrilled to hear from him.

"Hi, Giselle, do you have a minute to talk?" His voice sounded a little uptight.

Giselle frowned and looked around to see if Grandmama was nearby, but she was alone in the family room.

"Yeah, I do." She gulped.

"I had a call from Lusi. She's distraught, Giselle. She's in anguish."

Giselle remained silent while Uncle Mick kept his monologue going.

"She wants to make things right with you. She wants to talk and tell you her side of the story. Can you give her a chance?" he asked.

Giselle rolled her eyes. She bet her mum had made him ring her. "Did Mum tell you to ring me?"

"No. Lusi would be mortified if she knew I called you. Please, Giselle, just try to talk to her. Hear her out." His voice softened.

Giselle twirled the end of her side plait and bit her bottom lip. How could she tell him that she didn't want to see her ever again?

"I don't want to see her again." The words blurted out of her mouth before she had a chance to stop them.

"Excuse me?" Uncle Mick sounded confused.

Giselle gulped, and she took a deep breath. "I'm finding it really hard to talk to her right now. I just need time."

"Time? Time for what? She is your mother, and she deserves to be heard." He sounded angry.

"Yes, I know. But she lied to me!" Giselle snapped.

"Lusi has given you a home. A life."

"I know that!" Giselle exclaimed. She felt her head begin to pound. "I just don't want to talk to her right now. She has hurt me."

"Lusi has cared for you, and she's given you her love all these years. How could you forget that? Where would you be if she had not adopted you as her own?"

Giselle winced at his words. They stung.

"Life is hard, Giselle, and you must learn to accept it. There's no time for self-pity, and there's certainly no point in you shutting her out of your life."

Tears sprang in her eyes.

She heard Uncle Mick sigh. "I've seen you both together, and there isn't a mother-daughter relationship closer than yours. Biology doesn't make a parent, Giselle. It's the moments you share together."

Giselle shut her eyes as tears flowed freely down her face.

"I need to go. Please keep what I said in mind. I love you."

The click on the other end indicated he had hung up.

Tears continued to flow down her face and onto her top. His words—*Where would you be if she had not adopted you as her own?*—cut through her like a dagger.

Where *would* she be?

Giselle stood up, grabbed her phone and her tote bag, and was heading out of the family room when the box with the letters and photos of her as a little girl caught her attention. Grandmama had left them on the sofa from the other night. Giselle looked around, grabbed the box, and put it into her tote bag. She took twenty dollars from the money jar filled with coins and notes that Grandmama kept on the mantel. This jar was for times when they needed to catch the bus, pay a taxi, or just give to people who asked for donations.

Quietly she opened the front door, then called out, "Just going to the store to grab something." She tried hard to hide her tears.

"Okay, darling. Dinner will be ready in an hour. Don't take long." Her grandmama's voice was drowned out as she closed the door and bolted down the long driveway.

She needed to think, and she needed space.

Giselle checked her phone to see the time and noticed the battery was low. She grunted. Hopefully it would last long enough while she was at the lighthouse.

As she rounded the corner, she saw the bus about to leave. Lifting her hand, she ran and signaled for it to stop. Luckily, the bus driver saw her and waited until she got there. Huffing, she got on and thanked him.

Breathing out, she slumped on the seat. She felt bad not telling her grandmama where she was going, but she needed to get away for a few hours.

Giselle checked her phone again; it was 4:25. Good, it was still light, and the sun wouldn't set until seven. She had plenty of time to unwind and then go home, hopefully refreshed and able to think better.

She leaned her head against the bus window and was about to close her eyes when dark clouds in the distance caught her eyes. She sat up. It looked like a storm threatened. She gulped. *No, not a storm!* It was too late to go back, so she might as well get to the lighthouse stop and then catch the next bus back. Yes, that sounded like the perfect plan. She might just make it back to dinner in time.

She hoped.

Chapter 24

When the bus arrived at the lighthouse, Giselle hopped off and waited for the bus to drive off. She needed to cross the road and catch the bus back to Crest Pointe. The storm was coming, and she wanted to be home before it did. To her surprise she noticed that Charlotte Bay was bright and sunny without a single dark cloud in the sky. *Thank you, God*, she said to herself and paused. She hadn't talked to Him for a while and wasn't sure if she really could right now either.

She hoisted her bag on her shoulder and hurried up the steps towards the rundown but commanding lighthouse. Once she was at her usual spot, she looked over the horizon at the bluest of skies and ocean. She wished she could paint that scene right now—it was perfection. The breeze picked up a little. She lifted her face towards the sky, letting the cool wind blow through her face and hair. There was something about the ocean and this lighthouse that made her feel secure. Nonno always said that the strength and protection of the lighthouse was a strong tower like God.

"My little da Vinci," he would say, "always remember that God is a tower. Proverbs 18:10 says, 'The name of the LORD is a strong tower; the righteous run to it and are safe.' Don't forget to go to him when you see no way out of your problems."

"Okay, Nonno," she would say.

She didn't know why she was thinking about that now, but she knew she missed him more than ever. He had never treated her like an *adopted* grandchild. He treated all of his grandchildren the same.

Remembering the box of photos and letters she had bought with her, Giselle decided to have a peek. She wanted to prove Uncle Mick wrong. She was sure she would find something amongst the photos and letters that she could send to him showing that the only reason her mum had kept her was because her father had died.

Feeling a little angry, she abruptly opened her tote and lifted the lid of the box. Envelopes in different shades sat neatly piled on top of each other. Photos in different sizes were tucked underneath. Giselle reached for the first letter and then pulled her hand away. She couldn't do it. *Come on, Giselle,* she chided herself. *Don't be a wimp. Open it.*

She sighed and reached for the envelope again. With shaky fingers she opened the folded letter written in her mother's handwriting and began to read. She scanned the first few lines. Nothing interesting jumped up at her. Until she got to a sentence that brough back lots of memories.

My little Giselle and I made little flower wreaths today—we wore them on our heads like crowns and then we had a tea party. It was amazing. She is the most wonderful daughter anyone can have. I can't wait for Giselle to meet her Grandmama. You will fall in love. I am the luckiest mum in the world!

Clipped to the letter was a photo of Giselle and her mum—Lousiana. Both wore floral wreaths and sat around a little table adorned with tiny cupcakes and teacups. Giselle's little face was turned towards the camera, and a big grin decorated her face.

Giselle touched the photo gently. She remembered another time she had made wreaths with her mum. It was her eighth birthday party, and they were sitting on the grass together. They were making yellow floral wreaths for each of her friends who were attending. She had told her mum she wanted everyone to wear flower crowns. Her mum had been really excited about the idea. If there was one thing her mum loved, it was flowers. Her mum and flowers were always a good mix.

Putting the photo back in its place, she took out another letter. Letter after letter, Giselle read lovely things about herself. How much she was loved and what a great daughter she was. Another sentence caught her attention.

I never want to see her hurt again. It pains me that someone so tiny has been through the loss of her mum and dad. I desperately want to go home and bring Giselle to you. I know you will adore her. Her cousins will go crazy when they see her. She is a little fragile after Warren's death. She has developed an extreme fear of storms, and it frightens me how she screams. I don't want her to be hurting, but I don't know what to do. I need to be with you both. I want my daughter to grow in a strong Christian environment. I love her with everything in me. I love her like my own, and no one will ever change that!

Giselle put the letter away as she wiped the corners of her wet eyes. She blinked and looked out towards the water. Suddenly her eyes widened as she noticed the dark menacing clouds over the horizon. They were darker and thicker than the ones she had seen earlier. A sudden roll of thunder announced a big storm entering Charlotte Bay. Giselle froze.

No, this could not be happening. Giselle scrambled to pick up her things and decided to dart towards the bus stop and get home. She hoped she would make it to Grandmama's before the wild storm hit. The wind had picked up. It whistled around her ears and tousled her hair. Giselle could see people also leaving the lighthouse.

As she ran towards the bus stop, her phone rang. It was Sophie.

"Soph!" Giselle exclaimed, trying to keep her voice composed. "My phone's dying. I don't know if I can talk right now."

"Whoa! It's so noisy there. Where are you?" Sophie asked.

"At the lighthouse. A storm is coming and it's looking really dark already. I'm going back home."

"Gi, Dad called me and told me you're still not talking to Aunty Lusi. You're being unfair. She must be dying!" Worry laced her voice.

Giselle rolled her eyes. "She lied to me, Soph! You might not understand, but imagine if you suddenly found out Uncle Mick wasn't your real dad. Imagine how hurtful that would feel. You don't get it. No one gets it." Giselle stopped under a tree to talk. She felt angry that everyone was picking on her. Why didn't they blame her mum?

"It's not that no one understands, Gi. It's just that Aunty Lusi is upset and you should try to fix it. She is *your mum!*" Sophie emphasised the word as if Giselle didn't understand.

"Sophie, I hate that everyone is telling me to talk to *her*. You, your dad and even Grandmama. I've had it, and it hurts." Anger bubbled inside. If one more person told her to make up with her mum, she would scream.

"It's only because we c—"

Sophie's words cut off; Giselle's phone was dead.

Great, Giselle thought, *now Sophie will think I hung up on her.* She threw her phone in her bag and rushed towards the bus stop. A strong gust of wind blew through her hair. Another thunder echoed.

At the roadside, Giselle looked to the right and the left and was about to cross when a deafening thunder reverberated around her. Giselle screamed and covered her ears. Thunder echoed again, and tears sprang in her eyes. Why had she had the dumb idea to come to the lighthouse anyways? If only she had stayed at

Grandmama's. She knew she couldn't be at the bus stop while the storm hit. She should go find shelter. She scanned the area, and her eyes fell on the lighthouse. Another bolt of lightning flashed, and the skies opened; rain gushed from the sky. Giselle couldn't believe how fast the storm had hit. It was also quite dark. Running back up the steps, she held tightly to her bag. She squinted and tried to see through the veil of rain. When she arrived at the front of the lighthouse, she pushed the main door, but it was locked. She banged on it to see if it would open. It would not budge. Another roll of thunder boomed. Giselle squealed and ran to the other side. A little side door came into view. Her heart raced. She leaned over and pushed the door with force. It opened.

Relief rushed through her. She knelt and crawled through the little door. Her long, drenched hair caught on a sticky spiderweb.

"Ew, yuck. No!" Giselle fumbled and broke through the spiderweb. Once inside she blinked trying to adjust to the darkness. The smell of stale, stuffy, salty air tickled her nose, and she sneezed. She stood up slowly and pulled the sticky cobwebs from her hair. She wriggled and squirmed, shaking herself to make sure no spiders stuck to her clothes.

A roll of thunder clashed around the lighthouse. Giselle gasped and dashed to a corner of the room, where she sat quivering and waiting for the storm to pass.

Tears of sadness, loneliness, and fear overwhelmed her soul. She buried her face in her hands and sobbed. She cried for the loss of her Nonno. She cried for losing her biological mum and dad. She cried because Uncle Mick's words had cut right through her heart, and she cried because Sophie was disappointed in her. But her biggest tears came from when she thought about her mum. Her *adoptive* mum. The only mother she had ever known. The woman she truly loved with all her heart. The sound of monstrous thunder close by shook the lighthouse. Giselle covered her ears and screamed. She wished it would go away. She wished she was home, wrapped safely in her mother's arms. Tears burned her eyes as she thought about the woman she had called mum since she was two. More tears and more screams echoed inside the big, empty, dilapidated building as the thunder got closer and louder. Giselle looked up and gasped. It was dark. So dark she could barely see the palm of her hand.

Torrential rain bellowed from above, and Giselle trembled at the eeriness of the room. In the darkness Giselle stuck her hand in her bag and fumbled inside until she found her phone. She curled her fingers around it. Her hands shook as she tried to make it come to life. Oh no, she had forgotten it was dead.

She put the phone back inside the bag and stood up slowly. If she could get to the main door, she could open it and let some light in. She hated the storm, but she didn't want to be in total darkness. What if someone lurked inside?

Tentatively, she put her palms on the cold, rough walls and began to feel her way around the building. Another roll of thunder echoed but softer this time. Giselle trembled. Maybe the storm was passing?

She continued walking slowly. Then all of a sudden, as she took the next step, her foot tripped over something on the ground that made her tumble and fall on her knees. Giselle let out a yelp. She felt the roughness and pain on her palms and knees as she crawled across the uneven ground. Giselle extended her hand to grab onto the wall and stand up, but her hand hit empty air. Where was the wall? She reached again. The wall must be farther away.

The thick darkness engulfed her, and the sound of something falling nearby made her freeze. What was that? Someone was inside. Someone was going to kill her. Her throat tightened. Her breathing accelerated, and her body began to shake. Suddenly she couldn't swallow or breathe. Something small and furry scurried by her knee. Giselle whimpered. She opened her mouth to scream but nothing came out. Footsteps, shadows, and noise surrounded her. She became disoriented and felt like she would pass out. Another thunder boomed.

In her panic Giselle shouted, "God, help me, please!"

Tears streamed down her face as her Nonno's words came to her mind. *"The name of the Lord is a strong tower; The righteous run to it and are safe." Don't forget to go to him when you see no way out of your problems.*

Giselle closed her eyes and whispered a prayer. "God, I know I haven't talked to you in ages, but I need you. I know I've lied. I've been angry and resentful, but please save me. Please be my strong tower and help me." She kept her eyes closed and repeated the Bible verse over and over.

The words washed over her like a security blanket. Gradually, the thick darkness that had surrounded her began to dissipate. Her throat opened and she took big gulps of air.

"Thank you, God," she croaked.

Unexpectedly, loud banging echoed in the lighthouse. Her eyes popped open. She froze. Who was there?

The main door opened, and light broke through the darkness.

"Giselle? Giselle, are you in here?"

Giselle gaped. "Ma?"

"Stay outside. I will check inside *alone*. It could be dangerous," a man's voice ordered.

"I don't care if the building is falling, Devon; I need to find my baby!" Her mum's don't-even-bother-to-tell-me-what-to-do tone echoed in the eerie building.

"I'm going to look for her too, officer." It was the voice of her grandmama. They had come looking for her.

Giselle couldn't believe they were in the lighthouse. For a split second she thought she was dreaming. But the voices confirmed she wasn't. She wanted to shout that she was there, but weakness and nausea took over. She covered her mouth with her hand and breathed in slowly.

The light of the torch illuminated different areas of the building until it rested on her.

"She's here! I found her!" The voice of the officer rose in excitement, and Giselle closed her eyes in relief.

Chapter 25

"Giselle!" The voices of her mum and her grandmama echoed in the empty space as they rushed towards her.

The next few minutes felt like a blur. The officer checked around, then squatted and asked if she was hurt.

Giselle kept saying she was fine but felt weak.

Her mum and the tall, dark officer grabbed her from under the arms and stood her up. She buried her head on her mum's shoulder and cried.

"We better get out of here, ladies. This place is not safe. Something might collapse from within." The officer pointed his light to the never-ending ceiling and shook his head.

Giselle, her mum, and Grandmama followed close behind. Her mum wrapped her arm around Giselle's waist for support. A sprinkle of rain and the sounds of soft thunder were all that was left from the storm. They reached Grandmama's car, and the officer opened the back door. Without any words, her mother ushered Giselle inside, draped a towel around her shoulders, and closed the car door. Giselle wrapped herself up and watched as Grandmama and her mum spoke to the officer. She heard Grandmama thank him and say goodbye. Then she got into the driver's seat and buckled her seat belt. Her mum stayed back talking with the officer. She gave him a tight hug and darted into the back seat with Giselle. She glanced at her mum shyly.

"Oh, honey!" Her voice broke, and she placed a hand on Giselle's face. "I was terrified."

Giselle moved over and buried her face on her mum's shoulder and cried. She sobbed all the way to Grandmama's house. Her mum stroked her head and whispered calming words.

When they arrived home, Giselle was instructed to hurry upstairs and shower immediately and change into clean clothes.

The warm water seemed to wash not only the grime but also the anger and resentment she felt towards her mum. She could still see her mother's pale distraught face and the relief when she had been found.

She knew she had to apologise when she got downstairs. They had a lot to discuss.

After changing into clean clothes, Giselle walked slowly downstairs feeling a little nervous.

Peeking in the kitchen she saw her grandmama making tea. She looked up and smiled. "Oh, darling, I'm so glad you're okay." She put the kettle down and hurried to embrace her in a warm hug.

Giselle held on to her, not wanting to let her go. "Thank you for finding me," she whispered.

Her grandmama wiped the tear from the corner of her own eye. "I got a call from Sophie who told me she had been talking to you and the phone cut off. She told me you were at a lighthouse and a storm was coming your way."

Her grandmama shook her head and continued. "I know storms terrify you, so I called your mum. She called her officer friend Devon. They pretty much tore down the door of that place to see if you were there. We even looked in the water and the rocks below." She shuttered.

Giselle's stomach tightened at the anguish they must have felt; thank God they had found her alive.

"Darling, your mum's waiting in the family room. I'll bring you both tea and I'll go to bed." She gave Giselle a little push towards the family room.

Giselle bit her bottom lip. "I'm nervous. What do I tell her?"

"She is your mum. Just speak from your heart, darling. You will be fine." Her grandmama smiled and turned to get the tea.

Giselle took a deep breath and walked down the hall towards the family room. She found her mum taking out the contents of her bag to dry everything out. When she heard Giselle's footsteps, she turned around. "It's drenched," her mum said.

Giselle ran towards her mum, who opened her arms and held her close while she cried.

How had she been so dumb to almost lose the woman who had raised her and loved her as her own? The woman who defended her from anyone who said anything nasty.

The woman who loved her unconditionally. The one who made flower wreaths and went to all her school events no matter how unimportant they seemed. The one who had braved the storm to save her when she needed her most.

A deep respect and love settled in Giselle's heart as she saw her mum in a new light. Finally, she detangled herself from her embrace and flopped on the sofa as she dried her eyes.

"I'm so, so sorry I was so mad at you." Giselle's voice shook.

Her mother sat facing her on the sofa and shook her head. "You had every right to be angry. I should have told you everything a long time ago. My dad, your Nonno, told me to tell you. Then he threatened to tell you himself, and I forbade him to. I didn't want to lose you." She wiped her eyes.

"You wouldn't have," Giselle said.

"It's been so difficult keeping it a secret from you all these years. I have no excuse. No excuse at all." Her mum sighed. "After you lost your dad, I vowed that nothing would hurt you again. Not even the truth."

"Here's some tea for my loves," Grandmama said as she walked in with a tray, two mugs of tea, and a plate of cinnamon rolls.

Giselle's stomach growled, and they laughed. She had forgotten she hadn't had dinner.

She grabbed a roll and devoured it in seconds. Her grandmama kissed her head, then left.

"Ma," Giselle said, wiping her hands on a serviette and looking at her mum, "I have been lying to you too." She bit her bottom lip.

Her mum paused with her cup midway to her lips. "Oh?"

Giselle shifted in her seat. "I, um, I actually got a job behind your back and started working at Kim's café." She rushed on to tell her about the job and the motorbike incident. She wanted everything out in the open. As soon as she told the truth, she felt a huge weight lift from her shoulders.

"I see." Her mum tightened her lips and lifted an eyebrow.

"I really wanted a job so I could save and go visit Dad's grave. I didn't want you to be angry. You got so mad at me for asking that time. Remember at Uncle Mick's house?" Giselle shivered at how angry she had been.

"Oh, honey, I wasn't angry. I was afraid you were going to find out the truth. If you needed a passport, then you would ask me for your birth certificate and everything would be revealed." Her mum paused and ran a hand through her tousled blonde hair. "I guess all lies are found out in the end. God has a way of uncovering them, doesn't he?" She let out a nervous laugh.

"I understand if you want to ground or punish me or something." Giselle wouldn't blame her.

Her mother smiled. "No, I think we've both been punished enough with our lies and guilt. We both need to forgive each other." Her mum put her mug down and rubbed Giselle's arm. "Giselle, I'm not opposed to you getting a job. It was the documents I didn't want you to find. So you can go back to work if you like."

Giselle shook her head. "I think I was fired. I've missed a few shifts. But that's fine. I found out that I can't work and study at the same time. It's too stressful." She rolled her eyes. "I guess you *do* know best."

"The last few days have made me think a lot. I think we should go to London together at the end of the year. I can take you to all the places your dad and I visited. I can even take you to where we met. And you can visit both your parents' graves." Her mum paused; a sad look washed over her face.

Giselle beamed. "Yeah, I would love that, Ma. But this year? Really?"

Her mum nodded. "Why wait till you're in year twelve? I figure at the end of year twelve, you can go with your cousins like you planned. But we can go for Christmas."

Giselle clapped her hands. "Yes, yes. I would love that. Yes!" She squealed. Her stomach flipped at the thought of finally going to Europe.

"Giselle, I don't want to lie anymore. I want to tell you everything. I want to tell you about the death of your dad and how it happened. I'm done hiding the truth."

Giselle nodded.

"There was a huge storm when your father died in the car accident. We had been invited to a party and were driving there that afternoon. You were sitting in the back in your baby seat. I was in the front with your dad. He was driving fast and it scared me. That day hadn't been a good day for him—it was the anniversary of your mum's death. He wasn't dealing with it very well." Her mum wrung her hands as she recounted that awful day.

"I remember asking Warren to slow down. Telling him the storm was bad and he was driving too fast. He yelled at me and told me to be quiet. He said I exaggerated everything. I didn't want to argue with him, so I kept quiet. But he kept talking and shouting at how I was bothersome lately. I told him just to concentrate on driving and to lower his voice. His shouts and the storm outside were beginning to scare you, and you started to cry. He then went on to tell me that I was nothing like Olivia." Her mum's voice trembled. "It wasn't the first time he said that. Whenever your father was angry, he would tell me the exact same thing. It hurt me so much." Her mum paused. "I never tried to replace your mother."

Giselle's eyes bulged with the new information. She remained silent, gripped by the story, and pained as she listened to her mum.

"Anyway, he was driving so fast that the trees began to whiz past. Everything started to blur. You must have felt the danger because you started to tell him to stop. But he didn't. He lost control and we crashed." Her mum paused and looked out towards the dark trees at the back of the house. Her face so sad and forlorn. Giselle's heart ached, and she scooted closer to her. She grabbed her mum's hands in hers.

Her mother squeezed her hands and continued. "He died instantly." By now she had started to sob. She let go of Giselle's hands and wrapped them protectively over her stomach.

Giselle frowned.

"I was pregnant. I lost my baby boy," she said in a whisper.

Giselle gasped. "Oh, Ma." Tears welled in her eyes. "I'm so sorry."

Her mum forced a tiny smile. "Thank the Lord you weren't hurt at all. I vowed that no one and nothing was ever going to hurt you. Since then, I've never felt like the time was right for you to know the truth. I thought I was protecting you."

"My dad sounds awful, and he treated you so badly." Giselle's idol-bubbles of her father burst one by one.

"Oh no, honey, no! He wasn't mean at all. He adored you so much. He was grieving, and he didn't want to see a counsellor to get help. He thought I could take the pain away, but I couldn't." She pressed her lips. "He was a good man. And he loved you with all his heart. Never forget that."

A thought crept into Giselle's mind. "Do you hate him?"

Her mum's head snapped up. "Why do you ask that?"

"Well, you don't wear the little brooch he gave you. You gave it to me instead, and your reaction when I told you to put it on was over the top. Plus, the painting you got from him is also hidden and covered in the garage. And .. . you never talk about him. You have also hidden all your wedding photos." Giselle waited for her mum to reply.

"I was angry at him for years. And I resented the fact that I gave all my love to him. For years I mourned the death of my baby. But I don't hate him." She took a drink of her tea, a faraway look in her eyes. "It has taken years for God to teach me to forgive him. I'm slowly getting there."

"Do you think I'm scared of the storm because of that day?" Giselle leaned forward, hoping this was the answer to her fear.

Her mum nodded. "I'm 100 percent sure. It's a trauma."

Giselle threw her head back onto the couch. "Finally. Finally, I know I'm not nuts!"

Her mum laughed. "You're not nuts, honey. Oh and guess what?" Her mother's eyes gleamed.

"I think we should both go to counselling to work out some of our issues. You can work through the storm fear, while I work through my fear of driving."

"I love that idea, Ma!" She leaned her head against her mother's and sat in silence mulling over the last few days.

Giselle sat up. "Ma, I also want to talk to the counsellor about a nightmare I had for a while."

"What nightmare?" her mum asked.

Giselle filled her in about the locket, the affair she thought Nonno was having, and the woman with the strange hands. She also told her that her dad and even Nonno had appeared in the same dream.

Her mum sighed. "It sounds to me like you have meshed all your memories into one. When I married Warren, your Nonno and Mick went to the wedding. You had an instant connection with my father. It was love at first sight for both of you." Mum laughed. "We also all went to the park together a few times. It was the same park your parents used to take you to." Her mother shook her head. "The brain is a very interesting and powerful organ."

Giselle dried her eyes again. She didn't realise she still had tears left. Hearing about Nonno made her miss him all over again.

"Honey, we should go to bed. We need a good night's sleep." Her mum gave a loud yawn and rubbed her eyes. "I haven't slept in days."

Giselle cringed. It was her fault, of course. "Can I stay home tomorrow and finish my art assignment?"

Her mother nodded. "Let's wake up late and eat pancakes for breakfast. Yeah?"

Giselle giggled and leaned over to hug her. "I love you so much, Ma. I'm super glad you're my mum."

"And I'm glad you're my girl."

Chapter 26

Giselle woke up to the sound of laughter and the scent of delicious food wafting to her room. She frowned for a few seconds and sat up trying to focus her sleepy mind. When the events of last night poured in, she jumped out of bed, ran to the bathroom to brush her hair and teeth, then bolted barefoot downstairs.

Her heart raced as she remembered she had made up with her mother. Oh, how she loved her.

She followed the happy sound to the kitchen and walked in. Her grandmama was flipping pancakes, while her mother was sitting on the kitchen stool talking on the phone. "Don't hang up. She just walked in. I'll put her on."

She extended the phone, and Giselle hurried to grab it. "Who?" she mouthed.

"It's Sophie." Her mum stood up, gave her a hug, and went to help Grandmama.

Giselle walked out of the kitchen and to the back garden. "Soph?" she whispered.

"Oh, Gi, I'm so sorry I was a total dope when I called you yesterday. I am so, so sorry! Please forgive me?"

"Already forgotten, Soph. And I didn't hang up on you yesterday. My phone died," Giselle explained.

"I figured." Sophie laughed. "I was just super worried, especially with the thunder I could hear in the background."

"I can't wait till you come tonight." Giselle smiled.

"Me too! Daddy is back home, and he's picking me up from the airport. I'll text you when I get home." Sophie's voiced bubbled with excitement.

"Love you," she said before ending the call.

"Love you too." Giselle hung up and clutched the phone to her chest. She remembered she needed to charge hers. She hurried back inside and had a sudden brilliant idea. She dashed upstairs and grabbed her sketchbook. She needed to add the final touches to her art assignment. Her heart swelled with joy as she admired the finished product; it was absolutely perfect.

She grabbed the book and her mum's phone and rushed downstairs to show them her work.

"Ready to eat?" her mum asked. She placed honey, butter, strawberries, and blueberries in the middle of the table.

Giselle nodded and placed the phone down on the bench. "Yes, but first I want to show you both my completed art assignment. Well, my completed draft."

"The one you were stuck on?" her mum said, raising her eyebrow.

Giselle had complained so many times about it. She had mainly filled her mother in during their night chats on the veranda. She'd told her how she hated that assignment, but her mum had encouraged her to keep going.

"Do show." Her grandmama rubbed her hands together and waited.

"It's not perfect or anything. But at least I have it ready to show my teacher." Giselle held up the page and grinned. "What do you think?" She bit her bottom lip.

She watched their speechless reaction.

Giselle shifted her weight to her other foot. "Well?"

Her grandmama spoke first. "Darling, it's beautiful. You are a true artist."

Giselle looked over to her mum and waited for her to talk.

Her mum's eyes shone with tears. "It's perfect. I love it."

Giselle chuckled and turned the image towards her. She thought it looked great too.

She put her art book down and gave both women she adored a big squeeze.

"I'll be back. I'll go take this up and come back." She ran up the stairs and looked at her drawing one more time.

She smiled. The self-portrait definitely had a special meaning that represented her life.

Giselle had realised her portrait could not be just of herself. There were different women who had helped shape her. She traced the sketch with her finger.

Half the face of the portrait belonged to herself. The other half was Olivia's, her biological mother's. Around the image she had drawn entwined daisies, her mum's favourite. She had also added them into the wreath that adorned her head. She had finished the whole portrait with heart-shaped daisies over her heart.

Giselle sighed and closed the book. She looked up towards heaven and whispered, "Thank you, God, for being my tower."

Then she sped downstairs to eat breakfast with the amazing women she was lucky to call family.

Dear Diary,

The last few days have been upside-down nuts and like nothing I have ever experienced. Truly, it has been weird as so many secrets were revealed. Mum has been incredible; I'm so happy we have made up. I'm also super happy that Sophie is here and we are besties again (not that we ever really weren't).

Okay, so I was totally weirded out to go see Uncle Mick. But as soon as he saw me, he squashed me into a hug and asked me to forgive him. He said he had no right to get angry at me. Plus, Mum told him off for being rude to me. LOL. Siblings.

I also got a text from Jace who still wants to hang out with me. I think I will. Friends for now and see where that leads (scary and exciting)—Josh reckons he's way too old for me and because he's not a Christian I shouldn't hang out with him. Josh is so adorable. He wants to protect me. But I have to figure things out for myself. Jace is really sweet, so nice and super cute. I like him lots!

I'm also going back to school on Monday, after being MIA all week. I'm catching up with Indigo and Quinn and I can't wait.

There's so much to tell them! I also have to clear Nonno's name and Ophelia's. I asked Grandmama why Ophelia didn't like her. Grandmama said it's because they were always baking rivals. They always competed with each other at church events, seeing who was the best baker! Old people can be too funny. LOL.

Yesterday, I went to see Kim and Talia to apologise. I felt so bad that I messed up my first job and let them down. Kim understood. She told me that if I ever wanted a second chance at Kim's café to give her a call. Tahlia just nodded and didn't say much. But that's cool.

Besides, Mum told me I should definitely concentrate only on school for now. I totally agree.

I can't wait to show Mrs. Reed my final draft of my art project. I know she will love it. And it's finally done! Yay!!!

Once Mum and I are alone, I have tons of questions I need to ask her. I want to know who my other grandparents were. Are they still alive? It'll be nice to know. Maybe when Mum and I go to England I can meet them. I'm super excited at all the possibilities.

I'm extremely grateful that God protected me the other day inside the lighthouse. Mum's officer friend, Devon, told her that bad things have happened there before. Ugh, sounds awful! But God is all over my life and I'm thankful.

I've started my devotionals in the mornings again. It really brings me peace. I cannot stop doing them again. I realised that life is a complete rollercoaster and the only constant thing is God—my strong tower. Nonno always said that I needed to rely on God 100 percent. I totally agree.

I almost forgot to mention that Officer Devon came by to see if I was okay. He brought flowers for me and Mum. It was really sweet and interesting, Mum blushed when he gave her a bouquet. I need to keep my eye on this situation, whatever it is.

Anyways, I'm off to have dinner with Mum, Uncle Mick, and Sophie. Later tonight my cousins are coming over for a movie—I hope it's romantic. LOL.

—G

Giselle sketched a box of popcorn, a TV, and some hearts on her page and closed her diary. She walked over to her dresser and grabbed the locket. She opened it and gently touched the face of her mother. She smiled as she stroked her fat baby cheeks. She really did look like a baby boy in this photo. It was probably her bold head. Giselle giggled, closed the locket, and wrapped it around her neck. She liked having it close to her heart.

With one last twirl in the mirror, Giselle walked downstairs towards the laughter and the aroma of delicious Italian take-out food. Her heart was full and overflowing. God was truly amazing. She couldn't wait to see what the rest of the year would bring.

Questions for Discussion

(You can use these questions in your book club or even for your morning worship time. Grab a notebook and write your answers).

1. Why does Giselle long for her mum to find a job?

2. Do you think lying to her mother about getting a job is a way for her not to be like her mum?

3. When do you think lying for a good reason is okay? Is it ever okay to lie?

4. Do you think Rachel should have double-checked with Giselle's mum about her job before signing her paperwork? How?

5. Have you ever felt betrayed or lied to by a friend or family member? When and what happened?

6. How does lying effect Giselle's priorities?

7. Do you find it easy to lie to those around you?

8. Giselle was feeling stressed about her school assignment and was especially frustrated because it was for

art, her favourite subject. Have you ever been stuck or gone blank on an important task or project? How did you overcome it?

9. Should Giselle have also prayed to God about her school troubles, or do you think they don't matter to God?

10. Do you have people in your life like Giselle's Nonno who inspire and encourage you? If yes, who is it?

11. Do you try to inspire and encourage others?

12. Do you believe in love at first sight? Why or why not?

13. Do you think it was creepy that Jace had noticed Giselle and then waited for her one hour after her shift?

14. If you are a Christian girl, have you struggled with wanting to be in a relationship with a non-believer?

15. Should Christian girls date a non-believer? Why or why not?

16. What do you think of Jace's response to not wanting to go to church? Are you on Esmeralda and Emily's side or Katherine and Silver's in how each pair responds to this about Jace?

17. Is it okay to be friends with a guy you have a crush on? Do you think you could just keep things as friends?

18. Why do you think Giselle called Jace for help and not her friends or cousins?

19. Do you think Josh's advice to Giselle was good, or do you think he was being an overprotective cousin?

20. There are genuinely nice guys who are non-believers, so why is this one "little" thing about not believing in God such a big deal when they have other amazing qualities?

21. What do you believe started pulling Giselle away from her morning devotions that she loved so much?

22. Giselle was terrified of storms, and this fear controlled her. How does the Bible say we should handle fear?

23. Are there any Psalms or Bible verses that bring you comfort? What is it about them you find comforting?

24. Have you ever been in a situation where you have questioned God's plan for your life?

25. Why do you think God lets tragedies happen?

26. How did Giselle's secret affect her faith?

27. Do you think Giselle's reaction or treatment of her mum was justified? Or did she react impulsively? What would you have done in her situation?

28. Do you think Lousiana had a happy marriage? Why or why not?

29. Giselle called to God when she was trapped in the lighthouse, and she felt His peace. Have you ever been in a helpless situation where you called out to God? When?

30. Have you felt God help you, or are you still waiting? Explain.

CHARLOTTE BAY GIRLS

Silver and the Mystery of the Bells (eBook)

One day while looking for a Christmas nativity set in the attic, Silver stumbles across a jewellery box that holds a beautiful bell pendant. Something about that pendant looks familiar. Where has she seen it? And why does the lady from the jewellery shop act so strange when she asks about it?

There's a hidden secret, and Silver is determined to find out what it is. Except the truth will rock her world!

Available online as an eBook. Grab your FREE copy at www.gigistorylibrary.com.au.

Tune in Monday mornings to **'GIGI TEEN RADIO'**
on all podcast platforms.

About the Authors

Maes E. and Stephanie G. are two sisters who love a good Christian mystery that keeps you guessing, has a great ending, and teaches you about God. They also love working with teen girls and sharing their love of God through their podcast, their books, and their Bible studies. You can find out more on their website, www.gigistorylibrary.com.au, or email them at writegigi5@gmail.com. They absolutely love getting emails from their readers and will reply to them!